The Bookshop Mysteries

A BITTER PILL

S. A. REEVES

Published by Adventures in Writing.

https://www.adventuresinwriting.com/
https://www.sareevesfiction.com/

Developmental / copy editing, and proofreading by Edioak

Manuscript version 1.0
Build date: 13th September 2024

Paperback: 978-1-0687209-3-2
Hardback: 978-1-0687209-4-9
Ebook: 978-1-0687209-2-5

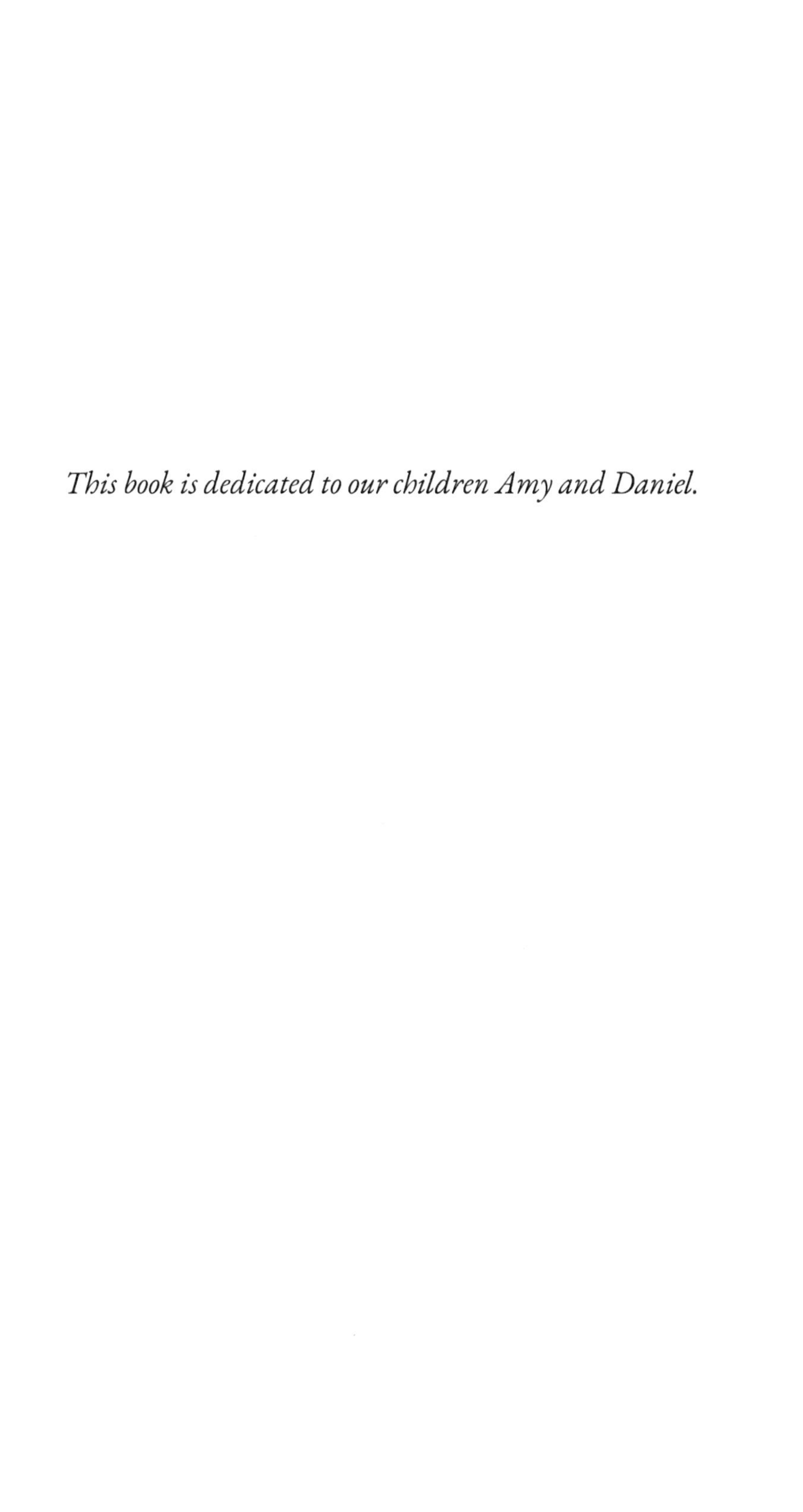

This book is dedicated to our children Amy and Daniel.

About the Authors

S. A. Reeves is the pen name of a husband and wife writing duo, who have been married for over twenty years. They are based near the Peak District in Derbyshire (United Kingdom).

They both like to read and watch murder mysteries, and will frequently stand in front of a whiteboard, plotting the perfect murder—for creative fiction purposes, of course.

This book is written and presented in British English.

This means for our readers in the United States, some words may be spelt different, such as favourite/favorite, behaviour/behavior, labour/labor, analyse/analyze.

These are not spelling mistakes or typos, it's just how us quirky Brits do things.

Join the Reading Club

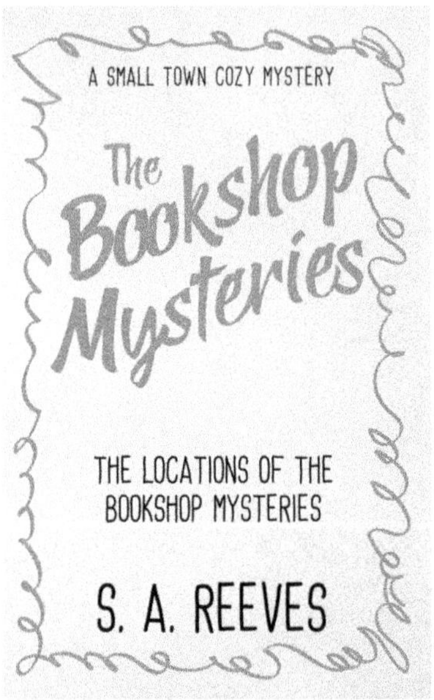

The Bookshop Mysteries is set in a real town, Belper (Derbyshire) in the United Kingdom, and is set in real locations. If you would like to see what these locations look like, then you can join our reading club to receive a free book: The Locations of the Bookshop Mysteries.

By joining the club we will let you know about new releases, special offers, and exclusive behind-the-scenes details about how we write the books.

https://www.sareevesfiction.com/join

The Bookshop Mysteries

Love the Bookworm Bookshop and Café? You can buy exclusive merchandise with the Bookworm's logo, from mugs, bags, t-shirts, hoodies and more.

Order from http://sareevesfiction.com
or scan the QR Code.

THE
Bookworm
– BOOKSHOP AND CAFÉ –

Contents

Chapter One

On an unusually pleasant spring day, the town of Belper awoke to the sound of the river Derwent whispering past the historic redbrick mill. Nestled in the heart of Derbyshire, the quaint little town looked like something gracing the cover of a souvenir chocolate box. Lush green hills and swaying meadows dotted the expanse, punctuated by cobblestone streets and brick houses. Belper was a portal to another, simpler time — a little pocket of countryside that the bustle of modernity had passed by after a brief sojourn.

Against this quintessential rural English setting, The Bookworm Bookshop stood proudly in the corner of the marketplace, its wooden sign swaying in the May morning breeze.

Inside, Gemma Curtis was a flurry of focused activity. Her brown hair was pulled back in an unruly ponytail, a few stray strands framing her face. With the sleeves of her jumper rolled up and her glasses perched on the bridge of her nose, she darted from shelf to shelf with an air of orchestrated chaos, making sure they were presentable.

"Morning, Ms. Austen," she chirped, slotting a well-thumbed copy of *Pride and Prejudice* into its rightful place among the classics. "And what are we doing here?" she quipped to a cookbook that had somehow found its way amongst the murder mysteries.

Over the next few minutes, Gemma carefully straightened a display of local history books, ensuring each spine was aligned with its neighbour. She stepped back, hands on her hips, proudly surveying her kingdom of paper and ink.

Perfect, she thought, a hint of a smile playing at the corners of her mouth. The Bookworm wasn't just a business to Gemma. It was a labour of love, an oasis for fellow bibliophiles seeking refuge in the pages of a good story. This was her world, and she was its curator, its guardian.

With a satisfied nod, Gemma slipped behind the counter, ready to greet the patrons of the day. After all these years, the gentle rhythm of each unfolding day was etched into her mind. She was familiar with each creak of the floorboards, each sigh of the shelves. And today, like every day, she would preside over the rustle of turning pages, the gentle chatter, and the hum of the coffee machine whipping up espressos and lattes in the café.

Perched on a high stool next to Gemma was Mavis Rawlings, her shop assistant. Steam curled up like smoky tendrils from the mug of Earl Grey that she cradled in her hands. The comforting aroma mingled with the musty perfume of books, and a whiff of lavender from Mavis's cardigan.

"Busy day ahead, dear?" Mavis asked, looking at Gemma over the rim of her cup.

"I hope so," Gemma sighed. At that moment, the shop door chimed open. A tall figure sauntered in, casting a long shadow across the polished hardwood floor. The man approached the nearest shelf and began browsing through it with a casual air. His fingers skimmed over the worn spines, never quite committing to extracting one and opening its cover.

"He's been here before. Bought nothing. Just watch," Gemma muttered out of the corner of her mouth, rearranging a pile of bookmarks on the counter. "He'll do his little dance, pretend to be interested, and then leave without spending a penny."

Mavis leaned in, observing the customer over the top of her spectacles. "You think he's one of those internet chaps? Buying books online?"

"Without a doubt," Gemma said with a wry smile.

"He considers the shop more of a showroom. It's all about the instant savings for him, not the actual experience."

They watched as the man paused, his head tilted slightly, eyeing a new release that Gemma had strategically placed to catch the light. The book was a recent bestseller that was still quite the rage, but she knew better than to hope for a sale on this occasion.

"Such a shame," Mavis clucked her tongue. "They miss the whole point, don't they? The feel of the pages, the smell of the paper, the triumph of a good browse ending in a find..." She shook her head.

As the customer continued his search, Gemma thought about new ways to entice readers into her store. There had to be a way to remind people of the wonder and charm of buying books the old-fashioned way. She was determined to find it.

Mavis rose from her seat with the easy grace of a woman who had spent years perfecting the art of customer service. She approached the man with a gentle smile, her steps soft and measured against the creaky wooden floor, and peered up at him through glasses that had slipped down her nose.

"Can I help you find anything?"

"Just browsing, thanks," the man replied, not bothering to take his eyes off his phone.

Mavis was undeterred. Her voice became even more warm and inviting. "If you decide on something, we have a special offer." She gestured towards a sign on the counter. *'Buy a book, and you get a discount in our café. Spend £20 or more, and there's a voucher for a hot drink of your choice!'*

"Thanks," the man said with a hint of surprise, as if the notion of additional value beyond the digital realm hadn't occurred to him. But it wasn't to be. He simply bestowed Mavis with a noncommittal nod before turning back to the shelf, and the indifferent ballet between thumb and screen resumed.

With a sigh, Mavis returned to her post. "Well, I tried!"

"Your efforts are always appreciated," Gemma said with a reassuring smile. "He might not bite today, but others will. And it's those customers we open the doors for every morning." Mavis nodded absently. Her gaze was fixed on the rows of books that lined the walls.

But Gemma herself was far from reassured. Her fingers tightened around the edge of the counter, her knuckles turning white as she watched the man tapping into his smartphone. He was oblivious to the world around him, completely absorbed by the screen.

Suddenly, Gemma noticed The Bookworm's blue price sticker on the book the man was holding, and then, her heart sinking, noticed the same title illuminated on his phone. "Mavis," she whispered urgently, "he's going to do it right in front of us!"

"Surely not," Mavis replied, adjusting her spectacles as if they'd let her see the man's intentions more clearly.

But Gemma's prediction unfolded with the inevitability of a well-thumbed novel reaching its climax. Her eyes narrowed as the man's thumb hovered, hesitated, and after a minute's deliberation, pressed "buy".

The man pocketed his phone and gave them a grin. "Thank you!" he said brightly. His insincerity stung more sharply than the lost sale. With a casual wave, he stepped out into the sunlit street, and disappeared from view.

"Cheeky so-and-so," Gemma muttered under her breath. Her brows were knit together in frustration as the door swung shut, the bell jingling.

"Typical!" Mavis sighed, her usual enthusiasm dimmed by the encounter. "It's like we're running a showroom for the internet!"

"Exactly!" Gemma exclaimed. "And it's hitting our sales hard." She leaned back against the counter, her mind racing through inventory lists and profit margins. "We need to brainstorm, Mavis. We need some fresh ideas to keep this place afloat."

"Something to make us stand out," Mavis echoed, reaching for her tea. She cradled the mug for comfort and inspiration. "After all, there's no substitute for a good old-fashioned browse and natter!"

"Right! Let's put our heads together. If there's one

thing The Bookworm is full of, besides books, it's creativity!"

And with that, they each took a determined sip of tea, the gears of innovation beginning to turn in their heads.

Chapter Two

Gemma twisted the lock into place with a resolute click, and flipped the sign from 'Open' to 'Closed'. It was the end of another underwhelming day for The Bookworm. Inside, Mavis was wielding a broom like a seasoned dancer. Sarah Hastings, a fresh-faced young woman in her mid-twenties was meticulously making the tables gleam for tomorrow's customers.

"Could we have a quick chat?" Gemma asked, her voice cutting through the quiet clinking and sweeping that was their usual closing-shop routine. Mavis nodded without hesitation, leaning her broom against a bookshelf.

"I'll make some cappuccinos," Sarah offered. She abandoned her cloth mid-swipe, and loaded coffee beans into the espresso machine. In a few minutes, the scent of freshly brewed coffee filled the air. Sarah deftly poured out three cappuccinos, and topped them with foam as soft as clouds. The trio sat at a table with their drinks.

"Business hasn't been what I hoped," Gemma began once they were settled, the warm cappuccinos cradled in their hands. "We really need some fresh ideas to draw people in. And fast."

Mavis made the first suggestion. "My dear, I don't really need the salary, you know. The pension covers me well enough, and besides, I also have the money Fred left me. And this," she gestured at the shelves, "fills my days. I'm here because I don't want to be rattling around the house by myself every day. The money doesn't matter to me, you know..."

Gemma quickly shook her head, the lines of worry on her forehead deepening. "Mavis, you're a gem, but I just couldn't..." The very idea of it was against her principles.

"Keep it in your back pocket, my dear," Mavis urged. "No offence would be taken!"

Gemma gave a grateful smile, unable to form words. For a few minutes, the three of them sat in quiet contemplation, nursing their drinks. Gemma knew the value of every individual's contribution. After all, it was at the heart of The Bookworm's charm, its identity. But while the offer touched her deeply, it was one she simply couldn't accept — not yet, anyway.

Sarah leaned back in her chair, her fingers tracing the

rim of her mug. "What if we were to rebrand ourselves a bit? Picture this," she said with a flourish. "Instead of calling the shop *The Bookworm Bookshop*, how about changing it to *The Bookworm Bookshop and Café*, or *The Bookworm Café and Bookshop*? It's catchy, don't you think? Makes it obvious that we are a café *and* a bookshop. Right now, people may not realise that they can pop in just for a cuppa and some cake. It might increase the footfall!"

Gemma tilted her head, considering the suggestion. The idea had merit. People would come in and patronise the café even if they didn't want to buy books, which would be good for business.

Yet, the thought of her beloved bookshop being relegated to second place behind lattes and lemon drizzle cake made her stomach twist. "It's really not a bad idea Sarah, but... well, I've always seen us as a bookshop first, and a café second," Gemma admitted, the words leaving a bitter taste on her tongue.

"Fair point," Sarah conceded with a slight pout. "But it might get more people through the door, you know? Branding is everything these days."

"You're right. I will give the idea some serious thought," Gemma sighed, chewing on her lower lip.

Silence settled over the three of them as Gemma grappled with the weight of making a decision. Suddenly, Mavis's soft voice sliced through the air, like a knife through one of Sarah's Victoria sponges.

"I've got it! What about inviting a writer into the store for an event? A reading and signing? That Dominic Westley, for instance. His book *Paper Boats in the Monsoon* was quite the hit. And well, people love a local celebrity!"

"Dominic Westley?" Gemma repeated, her brows furrowing. She pictured the suave author whose face had lately been plastered all across *The Guardian's* literature section. "That... could work. We have sold quite a few of his books recently."

"Exactly!" Mavis clapped her hands, her eyes twinkling with excitement. "People will come for him, stay for the books — and while they're at it, grab a coffee or a slice of cake. We'll sell out before you can say 'bestseller'!"

Gemma couldn't help but smile at Mavis' infectious enthusiasm. It was a brilliant idea, and it offered something more than just a temporary fix — it was an event, a new experience. She could practically see the shop buzzing with eager readers, the cash register humming with sales. Hosting these events regularly could be a great business idea.

"Fantastic idea, Mavis! Let's do it! If we can get Dominic Westley here, it could be a turning point for us!"

A faint hiss cut through the excitement.

"Sarah?" Gemma turned to look at the young woman. "You don't seem thrilled. What's the matter?"

Sarah set down her cappuccino, the froth still clinging to the rim. "Well, it's a great idea, and I can see it working for us in the long run but..." She sighed. "Well, it's just that that Dominic Westley is a bit, how do I phrase it, full of himself. Ever since that *Guardian* review, he struts around Belper like a peacock, all designer jeans and turtlenecks." Her nose wrinkled as if she'd caught a whiff of something sour. "One of my friends knows him, and he's really quite arrogant in person. The success has gone to his head."

Gemma nodded. She couldn't dispute the gossip. "True, he may be a little full of himself — but we can't ignore the fact that he's sold a mountain of books. And let's face it, he's the closest thing to a celebrity we've got here in Belper. Well, apart from that lady who acted in Coronation Street."

Mavis spoke up, her voice carrying a note of practicality. "I live near him, off Sandbed Lane. I could pop over and ask if he's interested. We've got nothing to lose, after all. And ego or not, I'm sure he would love the idea of reading to his fans." Her words seemed to sweep away any lingering doubt the other two had.

"That would be marvellous, Mavis!" Gemma shot her a smile. "If he agrees, I'll order another box of his books straightaway!"

"Actually," Mavis added, "we could sweeten the deal for customers. Buy a copy of *Paper Boats in the Monsoon* and get a 10% discount on any other book, along with the usual café discounts!"

"Fabulous!" Gemma clapped her hands in excitement. "This could be the first of many events we host here. Why didn't we think of this sooner?" This idea had truly roused her spirits – *The Bookworm* was going nowhere without a fight!

The meeting concluded on a high note. Together, the three of them tidied up the last remnants of the day's business, and with a final click, Gemma secured the lock on the door.

"Let me know how it goes with Dominic if you manage to speak to him," she called out to Mavis, who gave a reassuring nod and a thumbs-up as they parted for the day.

Chapter Three

Gemma was half-heartedly sorting a stack of newly arrived thrillers behind the counter. It was Wednesday, and the store was as quiet as a musty library on a pleasant summer day when the readers had run to park benches under shady trees. The tinkling bell announced an occasional customer, but most of the bustle was just Sarah, swishing about in the café serving up her signature frothy cappuccinos to the handful of patrons.

"Absolutely heaving, isn't it?" Sarah joked from across the room, her voice bubbling over the sound of the espresso machine.

"I wish," Gemma sighed, casting a glance towards the clock. It wasn't like her to wish time away, but she couldn't wait for word about Dominic Westley. Had Mavis talked to him? How far had the negotiations gone? They'd also need a bit of time to prepare for the book reading and signing. The thought of the event alone sent little prickles of excitement through her — it'd cause such a stir in sleepy little Belper!

Just then, the door creaked open, and a woman stepped inside. She scanned the shelves closest to the door, before making her way to the counter where Gemma greeted her with a smile.

"Can I help you with something?"

"Yes, do you have *The Stand* by Stephen King?"

"Absolutely!" Gemma led the woman through the bookshelves to the horror section. She reached for the thick spine, and presented it to the woman with the flourish of a waiter presenting his finest bottle of wine. "Stephen King's epic masterpiece!"

The woman's eyes widened. "Goodness," she said with a titter, "that's quite a reading commitment!"

"It sure is, but believe me, every page is worth the journey! It's one of my personal favourites."

The woman nodded, impressed. "I'll take it. And perhaps I'll be back for *The Dark Tower* if this one captures me."

"Excellent choice," Gemma said with a smile, walking back to the counter. "That'll be £12.99, please."

The woman fished out a crumpled ten-pound note and some loose change, while Gemma jabbed at the stubborn buttons of the cash register. The cash box refused to budge, and she gave it a good thump with her hand. A jingle of coins applauded her efforts.

"Looks like I need to add 'new register' to my shopping list," Gemma laughed, prying the drawer open further to deposit the cash.

"Or maybe just a stronger hand," the woman replied, chuckling as she collecting her change.

"Enjoy your read!"

The woman had barely left the store with her heavy book and a smile for Gemma, when the bell tinkled merrily again.

Mavis stepped into the shop, her cheeks rosy and glowing, both from the exercise of a brisk walk in the country air, and the exhilaration of good news. She made a beeline for Gemma behind the counter.

"Guess who's just made our little establishment the talk of the town!"

"He said yes?" The excited sweep of Gemma's arms caused a stack of bookmarks to scatter off the counter like autumn leaves.

"Dominic has agreed to do the event! He said he wants to do it next Tuesday," Mavis replied. "He was absolutely thrilled with the idea when I popped over last night!"

"That's wonderful, Mavis! Next Tuesday? That means we've got less than a week to get the word out." Gemma's mind raced with possibilities. She grabbed a pen, and started jotting down hurried notes on a scrap of paper. "I'll post about it on Facebook, print some leaflets... And maybe we could sweet-talk the local paper into giving us a mention!"

"Nothing like the rush of a deadline to stir the blood, eh?" Mavis chuckled, absently patting her hair into place. The very thought of a full bookshop energised her.

Their excited chatter drifted over to the café corner where Sarah was artfully plastering frosting on a sponge cake. Her ears perked up at the mention of Dominic Westley. "Hope you're planning to widen the doors for Dominic's grand entrance," she quipped, setting down her palette knife. "Or wait, that might not be enough. I think his ego will need its own postcode!"

"His ego can have a whole parade for all I care!" Gemma laughed. "This event is just the start, ladies. If we pull this off, we could make these readings a regular thing!"

"Any clue how many will turn up?" Sarah asked, brushing away a stray lock of hair. "I need to know how much cake to arm myself with."

"Hard to say, really." Gemma tapped the pen against her chin thoughtfully. "But let's err on the side of caution. Maybe throw in an extra Victoria Sponge and a batch of flapjacks. Those always go down a treat — and store well if there's any left over."

"Flapjacks it is," Sarah nodded. "If we run out, we'll

call it a success. And the next time, we could offer tickets to get an idea of the numbers."

"Exactly," Gemma agreed. The prospect of a crowded, bustling shop had lifted her spirits. "Let's give them something they won't forget!"

Gemma watched as Sarah returned to the café, and began cleaning the already clean coffee machine again. She let out a sigh of relief. How lucky she was to have such a good team on her side! With Mavis and Sarah's support and enthusiasm, she felt like she could pull off anything she set her mind to. Their first event at the bookshop was going to be an event to remember!

The thought of *The Bookworm* teeming with eager readers, and the soft murmur of literary discussions filled Gemma with a sense of purpose. An hour later, she stood at the door of the bookshop, surveying her handiwork with pride. The shop window was dotted with colourful 'Upcoming Event' posters.

"Next Tuesday's going to be quite the spectacle," she declared, more to herself than to Mavis, who had just finished straightening a row of classics by the door with her usual meticulous care. "Are you busy this evening, Mavis?"

"Oh, I'm never busy in the evenings," Mavis replied matter-of-factly.

"Baxter could do with a long walk, and I reckon we could hash out ideas for some future events."

At the mention of Baxter, Gemma's chocolate

Labrador, a warm glow suffused Mavis's cheeks. "I'd love that!" she replied. "Gets a tad lonely, it does, poking about the house on my own."

Gemma felt a pang of sympathy for Mavis, but quickly masked it with her characteristic cheerfulness. "Brilliant! I'll pick you up at six?"

"I look forward to it."

"We'll make an evening of it. I'll bring some cakes from the shop!"

"Oh, only if you avoid those treacherous walnut scones. They wreak havoc on my dentures."

"Noted," Gemma gave a small laugh, imagining the headline in tomorrow's *Belper Gazette*: *Local Bookshop Hosts Signing, Pensioner Loses Teeth*. "Just Baxter, some cake, and a good old brainstorm, then."

"Sounds perfect, my dear!" Mavis smiled.

Chapter Four

Gemma eased her small VW Beetle to a gentle halt outside Mavis's ivy-draped cottage. A quick glance in the rear-view mirror confirmed that Baxter was still sprawled out on the back seat. She gave the car horn a gentle toot — loud enough to let Mavis know she was here, but not so loud as to startle Baxter. It didn't work.

Baxter lifted his head with a jerk and perked up his ears. Inside the house, footsteps shuffled towards the front door. Locks clicked and clacked as Mavis emerged, her handbag hooked over one arm. She gave Gemma a warm smile and climbed into the passenger seat.

"Ready to go hiking?" Gemma grinned.

"Hiking? I was thinking more of a gentle meander," Mavis replied, securing her seatbelt with a decisive click. Gemma smiled, turning to look ahead.

With Baxter now sitting alert behind them, the car pulled away. Before long, they arrived at the Coppice carpark, next to the marketplace. The moment the door opened, Baxter bounded out with an enthusiasm that belied his years, his tail wagging like a metronome.

"Go on then, you!" Gemma called after the exuberant dog, following his lead. Together, the three of them descended the concrete steps of the carpark to join the flagstone path into the woods. They meandered along, until the path gave way to a dirt trail fringed by trees, their branches intertwined like old friends holding hands.

As they entered the woods, dusk wrapped around them like a shawl and the last of the light filtered through the canopy in dappled patterns on the ground.

"Isn't it just beautiful?" Gemma exclaimed.

"So it is! How lucky we are to have this right on our doorstep!" Mavis responded, awed.

With Baxter leading the way, they went deeper into the woods. After a few minutes, they had hit upon a steady rhythm. Gemma and Mavis strolled languidly along the winding path, talking intermittently about the shop and planning for the event, while the Labrador bounded ahead, and sniffed merrily at the undergrowth.

"Every time we come here, he acts like it's a brand-new adventure," Gemma remarked. Mavis smiled, her eyes on Baxter. "It's always the simple things that bring joy."

Gemma was struck by the wistful tone in Mavis's voice. "I've been meaning to ask something," she began. "Why don't you get out much, apart from work? I mean, you're always so lively at the bookshop, but outside of that..."

Mavis sighed. Her eyes were fixed on the amber hues of the leaves overhead. "Well, my dear, I don't know, really." Sensing her discomfort, Gemma attempted to change the topic, but Mavis continued.

"Ever since dear Fred passed away, I found myself... withdrawing from the world a bit. He was my world, you know," Mavis said, smiling at the memory. "We spent so many years together, did so many things. Without him, I just didn't feel like mixing with people anymore."

"But then you saw the advert for the Bookworm?"

"Exactly," Mavis replied, a spark igniting in her eyes. "Something about being surrounded by books and curious minds — it called to me. It brought me back into the fold, in a sense."

Gemma smiled. "I've always known that books have a way of bringing people together."

They continued in silence for a few steps, until Gemma's curiosity got the better of her. "Have you worked in a bookshop before? You seem like a natural."

Mavis chuckled. "Oh, heavens no! Before I retired, I was a business development executive at a large financial firm. My job was to explore new business opportunities — quite the challenge, I tell you!"

Gemma stopped in her tracks. Dear old Mavis, a business executive! "I never would have guessed! That's amazing!"

"Thank you, my dear. I was quite the executive," Mavis said, beaming. "And I've been thinking — perhaps there are a few tricks left up my sleeve that could benefit the Bookworm."

"Such as?" Gemma's entrepreneurial spirit was piqued.

"Event organising, for starters. I've got a mind full of ideas that could draw in more customers."

"Would you— would you take on that role, Mavis? Help us grow with events?"

"Really? Oh, Gemma, I'd be thrilled!"

"Unfortunately, I can't afford to pay more at the moment—" Gemma's face was sheepish.

"Oh, don't worry about that, my dear," Mavis interjected. "I won't accept any more money for this role. You know I love working at the store, and I've got my pension too!"

"That's settled, then," Gemma said, grinning from ear to ear. "Our very own events manager, Mavis Rawlings!"

"My suit and shoulder pad days are long behind me," Mavis joked, "but let me assure you, I'll give it my best!"

As they resumed their walk, the conversation turned to possibilities and plans. Baxter trotted back to them, his tongue lolling out of the side of his mouth as he panted.

Mavis delved into her well of wisdom. "You know," she began, "the Bookworm has so much untapped potential. We've got this charming, spacious shop that could host a myriad of groups. Reading clubs could use it for free — a community gesture, if you will — and we could offer the space to non-reading clubs to rent."

Gemma nibbled her lip, lost in thought. She'd always known her bookshop was cosy, but the idea of leveraging this charm in such a practical way hadn't dawned on her until now. It was humbling — and surprising — to see this savvy business acumen in Mavis. Gemma had thought of her as a sweet, slightly vague grandmother figure until now, not a former corporate woman.

"And let's not forget our coffee and cakes," Mavis continued, watching Baxter chase a squirrel. "We have quite good profit margins on them. It's all about creating an atmosphere. People pay for the experience, not just the products, you know. The *experience* is how you get people to come into the shop to buy books over and over again — instead of just pressing buttons on those infernal phones!"

"That's true," Gemma acknowledged. Her mind raced to take in all these possibilities. Without missing a beat, Mavis launched into another idea, her eyes shining with excitement.

"Oh wait! There's the Murder Mystery Club! They gather at The Swan pub in the evening, once every fortnight. The Swan charges an arm and a leg to rent the function room, you know. What if we offer them sanctuary at the Bookworm instead?" Her hand made an expansive sweep. "A low room charge, discounts on their selected readings, and a deal on refreshments. It would be a win-win, wouldn't it?"

"It certainly would!"

"And oh, my dear, you're a registered café already. So why not apply for an alcohol license?" Mavis suggested.

"Sell beer and wine from the café?"

"Yes! So that people who come to marketplace in the evenings can enjoy a little tipple."

"Lord, Mavis, that's never even occurred to me before!" Gemma mused. "Now that I think about it, that new hairdressers on the high street serves cocktails to their customers. Mavis, it's a brilliant idea! You're a genius! Do you think you can convince the murder mystery club to merge with us?"

"Leave it to me," Mavis declared, a mischievous glint in her eye. "I know Judith, the woman who runs the group. A little nudge, a promise of cosy armchairs, and she'll bring her flock over in no time!"

"That settles it, then," Gemma beamed, feeling a surge of gratitude for her friend. Mavis was truly an expert! With her experience, perhaps the Bookworm could be more than just a haven of literature — it could be a sleeping giant of community life. And together, they might just wake it up from its slumber.

Gemma chuckled as Baxter sniffed around the base of an old oak, blithely unaware of the master plan being concocting.

"You know, I don't think I've ever asked you about where you hail from, Gemma..." Mavis began. Gemma opened her bag and pulled out a plastic container. Inside were a couple of slices of carrot cake. She held it up for Mavis.

"Oh, lovely!" Mavis giggled. She picking up a slice and took a dainty bite.

"Well, I'm a North-East lass, born and bred," Gemma replied, her native Northumberland twang becoming a bit more conspicuous. "Moved down to Derbyshire for uni — I studied English Lit at the University of Derby." She smiled, thinking back to those days of endless books, and spirited late-night discussions about Shakespearean tragedies and post-modern novels.

"And after university?" Mavis prodded, stepping over a wayward root. Gemma took the other slice of cake and bit into it.

"Worked a few corporate jobs. Nothing that fed the soul, mind you. Then the redundancy came — honestly, it was a blessing in disguise. It gave me enough of a payout to buy the bookshop." Her eyes sparkled with the same fervour as the day she'd hung the 'Open' sign on the door of the shop. "Running a bookshop, it's always been my dream and now I'm living it."

Mavis nodded, a soft smile gracing her lips. "There's nothing quite like living out one's dream, is there? Forgive my prying, my dear," she hesitated, "but is there someone special?"

Gemma's amusement faded, as she recalled a part of her life she had done everything to forget. "I was engaged once... David, that was his name. He's a Detective Inspector in the local police."

"Was?"

"Yes. His job... it took a toll. Always at work, summoned at ungodly hours. As that went on, he became more distant. It put a strain on everything." She paused, kicking a small stone along the path. "In the end, I called it off. Still, we're on good terms even now."

"That's very mature of you," Mavis commented, patting Gemma's hand in a gesture of reassurance.

"Life goes on, doesn't it?" Gemma replied with a rueful smile. "Besides, who needs sleepless nights worrying when there's a shop to run?"

"Indeed." Mavis smiled. "And now, we have a murder mystery club to woo as well!"

The twilight cast long shadows across the coppice as Gemma clapped her hands. The sharp sound sliced through the quiet murmur of the night. "Baxter, come on, boy!" Her voice was firm yet melodious. With an enthusiasm that only a Labrador could muster, Baxter bounded back to them. He skidded to a halt at Gemma's feet, panting.

"Good boy!" Gemma scratched him affectionately behind the ears, as Mavis chuckled beside her. "Eager, isn't he? Like a furry whirlwind on four legs!"

"Absolutely," Gemma agreed, clicking the lead onto Baxter's collar. "Though let me tell you, it's more like having an overgrown pup than a dignified beast!"

They traced their way to the carpark, with brisk steps this time, the gravel crunching underfoot. Soon enough, Gemma's car came into view. Baxter hopped onto the back seat without prompting, settling down with a contented sigh, as though he'd never moved from there.

"Off we go then," Gemma said.

"Thank you, my dear, for such a great time," Mavis replied, buckling her seatbelt, her eyes filled with gratitude.

"Anytime, Mavis. I've really enjoyed it too," Gemma smiled, starting the engine. "Our little brainstorming sessions might just turn into regular outings for us — and for Baxter, of course!"

"Wouldn't miss it for the world!" Mavis beamed, her gaze lingering on the bookshop across the marketplace.

Chapter Five

Gemma stood outside the Bookworm, and drew in a deep breath to calm her nerves. Today was the day of Dominic Westley's event, and anticipation hung heavy in the air. Everything had to be picture-perfect, every inch of the Bookworm had to be spotless. She glanced at her watch. It was early still, but she felt every tick of the second hand.

Mavis arrived just moments later. "This will be quite the shindig, won't it?" she said mischievously.

"Let's hope so," Gemma prayed, opening the door and entering the shop. Sarah was already there, her bright yellow dress looking like a sunny blur as she flitted between the kitchen and the café front. She was baking an array of flapjacks alongside the extra Victoria sponge and carrot cakes that sat on the counter.

"Presentation is everything," Gemma called out to

her while arranging chairs into rows with a neatness that bordered on compulsive. It was the Bookworm's first event, after all — everything had to be just so.

By nine o'clock, the trickle of the first guests turned into a steady stream, and Gemma's worries of an empty audience evaporated as the shop filled with eager faces. Sarah, with her usual grace, served coffee, tea, and slices of cake, concealing her stress with a smile as the orders piled up. Gemma watched in amazement from a corner — her little shop had never seen such a crowd! People filed in seemingly endlessly, sitting down and waiting patiently after purchasing copies of Dominic's book.

"Looks like we've got a hit on our hands." Mavis gleefully rubbed her hands, her ever-optimistic presence exerting a calming influence.

But as the clock struck 9:30, Gemma began to fret, pacing back and forth. Where was Dominic Westley? The author's absence gnawed at her, casting a shadow over the much-awaited bustle. She fiddled with her necklace, watching the door with eagle eyes every few minutes.

At last, at 9:45, Dominic Westley entered the shop, looking every bit as dishevelled as a man could, while still maintaining an air of pretentiousness. His face was ashen, and his forehead glistened with sweat.

"Mr Westley, I'm Gemma Curtis." She extended her hand. "Are you alright?"

"Fine, fine," he panted, curtly dismissing her concern. "Just had to... rush over, that's all."

"Can I offer you some coffee before we begin?" Gemma asked, motioning towards the café, where the rich aroma of freshly brewed coffee lingered.

Dominic produced a flask from his coat. "I've brought my own, thanks. I'm rather particular about my coffee — a specific Colombian bean, farmed exclusively on a special, organic farm," he explained with a haughty lift of his chin. "This run-of-the-mill stuff just doesn't work to get my creative juices flowing."

"Of course," Gemma replied, biting back a smile. She couldn't help but find his fussiness amusing, though she kept it well-hidden behind a polite mask. As the restless townsfolk took their seats again, Gemma's nerves were replaced by pride. The Bookworm had come alive today — truly alive, just the way she'd always dreamt.

Gemma cleared her throat, and stepped forward with a practiced smile. The chatter of the assembled guests died down. The shop was filled with eager faces nestled among bookshelves that whispered tales of mystery and adventure.

"Good morning, everyone," she began, her voice steady despite the fluttering in her stomach. "I'm Gemma Curtis, the proprietor of the Bookworm. I want to extend a heartfelt thanks to all of you all for joining us today."

She motioned towards the heaving bookcases.

"Please take advantage of our special offer on books — for today only. And our café is open throughout the event for you to enjoy drinks and cakes. Believe me, the carrot cake is divine."

Amused titters were heard as everyone relaxed into their seats. With a gentle nod towards the guest, Gemma continued, "And now, without further ado, please welcome our guest of honour, Mr Dominic Westley!"

Polite applause escorted Dominic to his feet, and he adjusted the cuffs of his shirt before speaking. "Thank you, for that lovely introduction," he said, his voice smooth like silk. "It's an absolute pleasure to be here among such avid readers and supporters of the written word."

He paused, surveying the room with a smile. "My book, *Paper Boats in the Monsoon*, has been a labour of love — a narrative tapestry woven from the threads of human experience and emotion." Dominic's arms flew around expressively, as though he were conducting an orchestra.

"Indeed," he added with a tilt of his head, "it has been received rather well, if I may say so myself. The *Guardian* graced it with a four-star review — an accolade not easily earned, as I'm sure you'll all agree."

Murmurs of impressed acknowledgment came from the audience members. Some nodded in agreement, while others were clearly wondering if they should have read the review before coming here. Gemma watched from the side. Her lips were curled in a polite smile, but her mind busily noted every nuance of Dominic's performance. It was clear he relished the spotlight — he was positively basking in the glow of his own perceived brilliance.

"Enjoy the journey we're about to embark on together," Dominic concluded, holding his novel out like an emperor displaying a rare gemstone to his subjects. The room rang with applause again, warmer this time, as people settled in for what promised to be a morning of literary enlightenment — or at the very least, a good slice of cake and some juicy town gossip.

Dominic cracked open his novel and began reading. His smooth baritone soon reverberated in the cosy confines of the bookshop. The words on the page were dense, laden with symbolism and introspective tangents that would mesmerise James Joyce himself.

Gemma watched as the audience took in the words, some with their brows furrowed in concentration and others with eyes glazed over, lulled by the rhythmic cadence of Dominic's reading. She admired their dedication — it wasn't every day that one had to grapple with the labyrinth of modernist fiction before lunchtime.

A few paragraphs in, there was a sudden hitch in Dominic's voice. He broke into a cough. It was a minor disturbance, probably just a scratchy throat from the effort of reading — but it was enough to concern Gemma. With an apologetic smile, Dominic reached for his flask on the table, unscrewed the cap, and took a sip of his coffee. He attempted to press on, but his words faltered again.

"Excuse me," he stammered, a hand fluttering to his chest, "I must just—"

"Through there," Gemma interjected quickly, pointing at a door by the café, her instincts tingling. He gave her an imperceptible nod.

"Thank you. I apologise, everyone. I will be back in a moment." He strode across the room urgently.

Five minutes ticked by in silence, and with each interminable second, Gemma's concern transformed into full-blown worry. A glance at Sarah, who was biting her lips and twisting her apron in her hands, told her she wasn't alone.

"Shall I check?" Sarah finally whispered and, without waiting for a response, made her way towards the toilet.

The scream that pierced the air moments later was so jarring that several cups clattered against saucers. Gemma made a desperate dash towards the source of the commotion.

Her blood froze as she skidded to a halt outside the toilet door. Dominic Westley was sprawled on the cold tile floor, motionless and white, while Sarah stood by with her hands over her mouth.

"Something's wrong with Dominic!" Gemma cried out, bolting towards the counter. The hushed murmurings of the crowd suddenly burst into a cacophony of concern.

"I'm a doctor!" a man announced with calm authority. He went towards the toilet with Gemma close at his heels, clutching her phone. He bent down and checked Dominic's pulse.

"Call for an ambulance. Tell them it's a cardiac arrest," he instructed, kneeling beside Dominic's still form.

Gemma made the call, her voice trembling, her palms sweaty, as she relayed the address to the emergency operator. Her eyes remained fixed on Dominic's unresponsive figure — Belper's very own literary star was now the centre of a very different drama.

The doctor did all he could. He kept checking the pulse for any signs of life, and his hands pressed rhythmically against Dominic's chest in a desperate bid for revival. Time seemed to slow down to a crawl. Each passing minute felt like an hour. Gemma watched, her fingers knotted together, as the wail of a siren reached a crescendo outside, and paramedics burst through the door towards Dominic.

They urged everyone to move out of the way as they took over from the doctor, and switched to a defibrillator, shocking him several times. Eventually, they loaded Dominic onto the stretcher with swift precision. Gemma found her voice just long enough to explain his pallor upon arrival and his abrupt retreat to the bathroom.

Gemma and Mavis trailed behind the stretcher as it was wheeled out, right up until the doors of the ambulance slammed shut. As the vehicle sped away, lights flashing and the dwindling siren upending the morning tranquillity, Gemma felt a hollow dread in her chest.

Back inside, the Bookworm seemed to have morphed into a stage set, with utter shock and disbelief etched on every single face. "Thank you all for coming here today." Gemma's voice was strained. "Under the circumstances, I think it's best we close for the day."

She turned to the doctor who was gathering his coat. "Do you think he'll make it?" she asked. The question felt futile on her lips.

His answer was gentle, but noncommittal. "His pulse was very weak. It's hard to say what's going to happen."

The room deflated further at his words, as if a collective breath was released in silent despair. The doctor glanced at the trio of women — Gemma, Mavis, and Sarah. "Are you all okay?" he asked.

"We're... in shock, naturally," Gemma admitted, the reality of the situation finally hitting her like a frosty wind.

He recommended sugary tea and cake, the simplicity of the prescription feeling almost comical. "Sit for a while, then head home," he said, taking his leave.

Gemma watched him go. She would have to lock up, sort out the aftermath — but not before ensuring everyone had a moment to breathe, to sip tea, to absorb this surreal start to their day.

Gemma stepped over to the shop door, her fingers trembling as she turned the key in the lock. With a soft click, she flipped the sign to 'closed' and headed back to the others. The café, buzzing with excited conversation only an hour ago, was now subdued and forlorn.

Sarah was hunched over a table. Tears streamed down her cheeks, and her hands were clasped in her lap. Gemma approached, pulling out a chair which squeaked across the floor. "Sarah, my dear, are you okay?"

"I'm so sorry," Sarah sniffled. "I've never seen anyone—like that—" she stammered through her sobs.

"Hey, it's alright, I'm sure he'll be okay," Gemma said, gently rubbing Sarah's trembling shoulder. "You're allowed to be upset. It's a normal reaction to such a shock. Can I give you a lift home?" She was ready to do anything it took to relieve the young woman's distress.

"No, thank you. I think I need to walk, clear my head."

"Alright, but at least have some tea first," Gemma suggested, noting the way Sarah's hands were shaking. "It might help calm your nerves a bit."

Sarah managed a small nod as Mavis, bustling around with a teapot, poured out three strong cups.

Gemma caught Mavis's eye. Worry was clearly visible

in every crevice of the elder woman's face. She quietly accepted the cup handed to her. "I can't help but feel guilty, Mavis. Dominic looked so pale when he came in. Maybe I should've insisted he sat down instead of just starting the reading straightaway."

"You mustn't blame yourself, my dear. It won't do." Mavis's voice was firm. "He said he was fine. After all, you aren't a mind reader, nor a doctor. We had no way of knowing."

Gemma nodded. She sipped the sweet tea and let the warmth seep through her body. Mavis was right — they had all been blindsided by the sudden tragic turn the morning had taken. But as the shopkeeper and host, Gemma couldn't shake the nagging feeling that she should have done something more.

Chapter Six

Gemma arrived at the Bookworm bright and early the next day. She flitted here and there, organising a new shipment of books, and rearranging the shelves. She even wiped down the café tables. Emily, the Saturday assistant in the café, was busy brewing coffee and setting out pastries for the morning rush. Gemma was glad to have the extra help — Sarah had called in sick after the shock of the day before.

The bell announced an early visitor. "How are you holding up?" Mavis asked, hanging up her coat on the rack behind the counter.

"Fine, I think. Poor Dominic..." Gemma said with a dejected shake of her head. "I just wish yesterday had been a success. As things turned out, it's probably made business worse!" She looked glum.

"Nothing we could do about it, my dear. But at least

people will be talking about us, you know. Even if under tragic circumstances," Mavis said, patting Gemma's arm.

"But I've got an idea to cheer you up. It just came to me on the way here. How about a parents' coffee morning? We'll invite parents to come in for a quiet hour of coffee and cakes while I read stories to the little ones!"

"That's a lovely idea!"

As Gemma walked over to the counter, Emily brought over a fresh cup of coffee. The aroma of the brew filled the air. Gemma took a sip, and the rich flavour revived her spirits.

"Thanks, Emily," she said with a grateful smile.

"Anytime," Emily said, beaming. "You know, what happened to that writer yesterday... it's terrible."

Gemma shuddered at the thought of Dominic Westley's motionless body lying on the bathroom floor. She had known him only briefly, but the whole incident felt truly tragic. She still hadn't completely shaken off her guilt.

"Do you know if he is okay?" Emily asked curiously.

Gemma shook her head. "I haven't heard anything since the paramedics took him away." Emily looked thoughtful for a moment. Then she gave a sympathetic nod and returned to her work.

Turning her attention to the shop window, Gemma saw a police car parked in marketplace. The next moment, the bell chimed and two uniformed policewomen stepped into the bookshop. Gemma walked up as they introduced themselves to the bookstore at large: Police Constable Smith and Sergeant Nicholls.

"Morning', Gemma," Sergeant Nicholls said with a smile. "How are you holding up?"

"Hello, Fran," Gemma replied, tucking a loose strand of hair behind her ear. The Sergeant's presence had brought an air of officialdom to the room, and Gemma felt unaccountably nervous. "I'm managing, thanks. And how's Dave these days?"

"Grumpy as ever," Sergeant Nicholls chuckled, her keen eyes running over the shelves before settling back on Gemma. "You know, maybe you should take him back. Might cheer him up a bit — and more importantly, make the station a little more cheerful."

Gemma laughed. "Well, we'll just have to hope he finds happiness some other way. How can I help you?"

Sergeant Nicholls cleared her throat, and her expression turned business-like. "We're here regarding Dominic Westley," she said. The levity of a moment ago vanished completely. "I'm afraid I have some bad news."

Gemma could feel Mavis tense up beside her. "What happened?"

"Mr. Westley passed away, in the ambulance itself. It was all very sudden."

"Passed away?" Gemma repeated, rendered speechless from shock. Her mind harked back to the chaos of the previous day — Dominic's pale face, his clammy forehead. She looked at Nicholls searchingly. "But... was there something we could've done? Anything at all?"

"Unfortunately, no," Nicholls replied. "Even though a doctor was present, nothing could've been done to save him."

The words hung heavy in the air. Death, utterly unexpected and yet so...final. Gemma could barely process the reality of it all. Dominic Westley, with his snobbish words and his quirks and his pompousness — gone just like that. The reality of sudden death, so out of place against the warmth and serenity of the Bookworm, settled over her like a cold shroud.

Gemma fidgeted with a bookmark she'd picked up from the counter. Her hands simply needed something to do. "Can we help with your enquiries?" she asked vaguely. "Is— is there any suspicion of foul play?"

"Can't comment on that yet, I'm afraid," Sergeant Nicholls responded with a professional neutrality. "We're just carrying out routine enquiries after informing Mrs Westley, his estranged wife, of his passing."

"Poor thing," Gemma sighed.

"Could you walk us through what happened yesterday?"

"Of course," Gemma began. "We had scheduled an author reading and signing for his book *Paper Boats in the Monsoon*. Dominic was supposed to arrive at half-past nine but didn't show up until a quarter to ten.

When he eventually came, he looked rather unwell — pale and clammy, you know, like someone who'd just seen a ghost."

"Did you speak to him about it?"

"Yes, I asked him if he was feeling alright." Gemma mimicked her previous concern, a hand fluttering to her chest at the memory. "He just brushed it off. Said he'd been rushing to get here."

"Go on," Sergeant Nicholls urged, as Constable Smith took out her pen and notebook, and started writing.

"Well, he began his reading," Gemma continued, trying to recall the scene as vividly as possible. "But he couldn't seem to get through it. He kept coughing, stopped a few times, and then—"

"Then?" PC Smith prompted, motioning with the pen.

"He took a swig of coffee from his flask and tried to carry on," Gemma said, gesturing to where the flask had been on the counter. "A few minutes later, he excused himself rather abruptly and rushed to the toilet."

"Thank you, Ms. Curtis. You've been very helpful." PC Smith offered a small smile.

Sergeant Nicholl's eyes had narrowed at the mention of the flask. "You talked about a flask, Gemma. We didn't find one on Mr. Westley's person. Do you have it here, by any chance?"

"Actually, yes. He brought his own coffee — said it

was a special brew, from some exclusive Colombian farm. I found it a bit odd that he bought his own when we are a café and a bookshop, but oh well. Writers *are* a little quirky, I suppose." She chuckled wryly at the memory of Dominic's pompous description of his preferred beverage.

"Where is this flask now?"

"Behind the counter." She quickly went to the cash register and fished under it. Her fingers closed around the cool metal, and she placed it on the counter with a clink.

Without a word, Sergeant Nicholls produced an evidence bag. She picked up the flask gingerly and slipped it into the plastic, sealing Dominic's last sip away from the world.

"Thank you for your cooperation," Sergeant Nicholls said, nodding towards Gemma. "We'll be in touch if we need any further information."

"Of course. Have a good day, Sergeant Nicholls, Constable Curtis."

The little bell above the door signalled the officers' exit. Gemma watched as they got quickly into their car and drove off.

"Can you believe that, Mavis?" Gemma turned to her friend, whose thoughtful gaze was fixed on the counter, where the flask had been. "It's so sad!"

Mavis offered no reply, except a simple nod.

Chapter Seven

Gemma frantically unloaded her trolley at the checkout of Costco Wholesale in Derby, the closest city to Belper. The café was running low on coffee beans, something Sarah had just discovered when she came back in that morning. Gemma had to rush out to buy more beans, and also stock up on teabags, a selection of cakes, and biscuits. But Costco had been positively bustling — and she'd queued for twenty-five minutes before finally reaching the checkout. Gemma felt absolutely harried. It was like the sleepy charm of the Bookworm had been replaced by chaos, ever since... the incident.

As the checkout assistant scanned the items, Gemma came back to herself with a jolt. She quickly made the payment and was finally about to push the trolley to the carpark, when she felt a tap on her arm.

"Excuse me, are you Gemma? From the Bookworm in Belper?" a woman asked.

Gemma turned to face the stranger. "Yes, that's me. Can I help you?"

The woman introduced herself as Donna Westley, Dominic's estranged wife. Gemma scanned her with a sympathetic interest. What must she be going through, poor dear! Donna was about the same height as herself, wearing jeans, and a white t-shirt that was covered in a red and blue blouse.

"I'm sorry for your loss," Gemma said. "Would you like a coffee?" She offered earnestly. She'd sensed that the tension between them must be diluted with some normalcy.

Donna hesitated for a moment before replying. "Yes, please, that would be nice."

They made their way to the café tucked in the corner of the store. Gemma ordered two cappuccinos, making small talk about the weather and the store's excellent selection of pastries. She hoped to ease into the conversation without putting her foot on a landmine.

When their coffee finally arrived, Donna wrapped her hands around the warm cup and let out a grateful sigh. "I can't thank you enough for being there," she began, her voice steadier than before. "For calling the ambulance when Dominic... when it happened."

Gemma offered a comforting smile. "It was the least I could do."

Donna took a sip of her coffee, gazing into the distance through the floor-to-ceiling window before turning back to Gemma. “We had our troubles, Dominic and I. We separated nine months ago because — well, because he was having another affair,” she blurted out.

The word 'another' didn't elude Gemma. So, this wasn’t the first one he’d had. Certainly not a ringing endorsement of his character. “Oh, I’m so sorry to hear that,” she murmured.

“He wasn’t perfect, far from it. But we were going to try again. He assured me he wasn’t seeing anyone else. I — I was going to move back in with him.” Her voice broke at the last sentence.

Gemma observed the play of emotions across Donna’s face. Regret, sorrow, and perhaps just a hint of relief? It wasn’t her place to judge. She wanted to ask more, to understand the dynamic between Dominic and Donna. But this wasn’t the right time. So she just sat there and listened, holding space for the grieving woman.

“Anyway,” Donna continued, brushing away a stray tear with the heel of her hand, “I’m waiting for the pathologist to release his body. They said it should be today or tomorrow.” The practicalities seemed to give her a sense of control in a world that had suddenly turned upside down. “The funeral will hopefully take place next week. You are more than welcome to come...”

"Thank you, I would like that," Gemma said, her own emotions subdued. "Could I also bring Mavis, my assistant at the bookshop? She knew Dominic. In fact, it was Mavis who invited him to read at the store. She'd want to pay her respects."

"Of course, she's welcome too. It would mean a lot to have you both there."

Gemma rummaged in her purse. "Here," she said, handing Donna a business card. "That's my number, right there. Call me if you need anything, or even if you just fancy a chat." She smiled at Donna in a way that she hoped was comforting.

Donna took the card and tucked it into her handbag with a small smile of gratitude. "I might just do that," she replied. "Especially since I'm still planning on moving back to Belper."

"Anytime."

They exchanged farewells and parted ways, each pushing their respective trolley through the sliding doors of Costco.

Back at the Bookworm, Gemma found Mavis meticulously reorganising and dusting a shelf of romantic comedies, each of her movements precise and unhurried. A scent of lemon polish lingered in the air.

“Guess who I bumped into at Costco?” she announced, putting down the supplies on the counter.

“Who?” Mavis asked without turning around.

“Dominic’s wife, Donna.” The duster paused mid-swipe. Mavis swung round to face Gemma. “She invited both of us to the funeral next week.”

“Ah.” Mavis finally placed the duster down. “I would be happy to attend with you.”

Sarah, who had come over to collect Gemma’s delivery of coffee beans, looked up at the mention of the funeral.

Gemma turned to her. “Would you like to come with us? To the funeral?”

A flicker of surprise crossed Sarah’s face. Her lips parted slightly, before she composed herself. “Oh, um, no, thank you,” she stammered, her hands fidgeting with a napkin. “I didn’t know Dominic. It doesn’t really feel right for me to be there.”

“Of course, that’s perfectly fine.” She gave an understanding nod, then turned to Mavis. “It will be just us then.”

“Indeed,” Mavis said, picking up her duster once again.

Chapter Eight

Gemma's VW Beetle made its way slowly down the road, its engine purring like a contented cat on a sunny windowsill. Mavis sat beside her, a dignified figure swathed in black, her hands folded in her lap. Her gaze was fixed ahead, but Gemma could see the tell-tale glisten of emotion in her friend's eyes.

"It's such a sad day," Mavis murmured as they approached the Belper Cemetery and Chapel.

"It is indeed," Gemma agreed, navigating the car into a parking spot. She turned off the ignition and looked out at the cemetery through the window, taking in the sight of the lush green fields that stretched in the distance. The ancient chapel stood weather-beaten but erect, its spire reaching towards the heavens, as if in silent tribute to those that rested in its shadow.

The two women stepped out of the car, their heels sinking into the soft earth, and made their way towards the gathering mourners. It was a sunny spring morning, one that would normally have all of Belper out rejoicing. But today, the chirping birds and swaying blossoms only increased the desolate mood that pervaded the air.

Gemma spotted Donna, standing alone at the entrance of the chapel. Her black veil did little to hide her pallid face and swollen eyes. Gemma took Mavis by the elbow and guided her towards the chapel.

"Hello, Donna," Gemma said, her voice low and respectful. "This here is Mavis Rawlings. She works with me at the bookshop and was the one who invited Dominic to the bookstore. She was there the day Dominic passed away."

"Thank you both for coming," Donna said, her voice barely a whisper.

Mavis smiled.

Before more could be said, the solemn procession of the hearse drew everyone's attention. The polished black vehicle came to a stop by the chapel gates a little way from them, and the pallbearers extracted the coffin. Gemma felt a lump in her throat as she followed the mourners inside.

The church music began, the organ's solemn wail evoking a melancholic reverence. A moment later, the pallbearers walked down the aisle, holding the gleaming coffin aloft. Gemma couldn't help but think of

Dominic's last novel, a story about ephemeral things being swept away by an unstoppable force. It seemed almost cruelly ironic now.

The reverend took her place at the pulpit, and welcomed everyone with a solemn greeting. She spoke of Dominic's talent, his success as a writer, and his devotion as a husband, though Gemma knew the latter point was contentious, given his history.

The moment the reverend had uttered her last words, a stifled snigger rang through the sombre air. Gemma's head swung towards the back of the chapel. *Who would dare?* she thought. But the culprit's identity remained hidden amidst the shadows of discretion. Perhaps Dominic's philandering wasn't such a secret.

Trying not to dwell on the interruption, Gemma turned her attention back to the service. As the reverend proceeded with her sermon, she glanced to her right. Mavis was sitting upright and motionless, with tears in her eyes that she tried her best to conceal. She reached out and squeezed Mavis's hand, a wordless gesture of support — this was probably the first time Mavis had attended a funeral since her husband's passing.

As the last of the reverend's words echoed through the chapel, a morbid hush fell upon the congregation. It was so quiet Gemma could make out the muffled sounds of birdsong from outside. The service was drawing to a close, and one by one, people rose from the polished pews, their faces reflecting a sense of farewell.

Donna Westley, stoic in her grief, stood at the entrance, murmuring "Thank you" to the stream of attendees filing past. Her eyes were swollen from crying, and her gratitude seemed genuine, if delivered a little mechanically.

"Let's make our way out," Mavis whispered.

Gemma nodded, her gaze sweeping the periphery of the gathering. That was when she saw her — the lone figure of a lithe woman, half-hidden behind an ancient yew tree. "Who's that over there?" Gemma's question was soft, meant only for Donna's ears.

Donna followed Gemma's eyes, and her lips pressed into a thin line. "That would be Ellie," she said, her voice taut. "One of Dominic's... acquaintances."

"She shouldn't be here," Donna added with a defiant lift of her chin. It was clear she had little patience for the woman who'd brought about a rift in her marriage.

"Ah..." Words failed Gemma. After all, what could one say in such a situation?

Fortunately for her, the groundsman gestured for the congregation to follow him across the lawn towards the burial plot.

Mavis tugged at Gemma's sleeve. "Look there," she said, pointing towards a shadowed alcove where a teenage boy loitered. His black hoodie was pulled up, obscuring his face, and his baggy jeans hung low on his hips.

Gemma squinted, trying to place the faceless youth. "Do you know him?"

"Can't say I do," Donna replied, overhearing the exchange. She peered at the boy with a mix of curiosity and irritation. "Probably just some local kid, or a fan of Dominic's work, I suppose. Came here to pay his respects."

The boy seemed to sense their scrutiny, for he ducked his head lower still.

"Should I go over and talk to him?" Gemma pondered aloud.

"Probably not a good idea," Mavis cautioned. "Anyone that determined to hide their face at a funeral would probably not welcome the intrusion."

"Right..." Gemma felt a prickle of unease. There was something unsettling about the boy's demeanour, something that she didn't quite trust.

Exchanging a curious glance, Gemma and Mavis followed the others, leaving the mysterious figure all to himself. The clicking of their heels on the gravel path punctuated the silence as they prepared to bid their last goodbye.

The sombre procession made its way to a quiet corner of the cemetery, where headstones marked long-forgotten names and stories. The pallbearers walked with synchronous steps, their hearts and shoulders equally weighed down by the burden they carried. As they reached the grave, there was a silent mark of respect for Dominic.

The reverend stood poised at the foot of the open grave, her robes flapping in the pleasant spring breeze. She began the rites with a voice that seemed to wrap itself around the gathered mourners, soft yet firm and unwavering.

"In the sure hope of the resurrection to eternal life through our Lord Jesus Christ, we commend to Almighty God our brother Dominic, and we commit his body to the ground."

"Earth to Earth." The coffin descended into the grave. Donna's sobs rose above the reverend's words, raw and unrestrained. Gemma placed a comforting hand on Donna's convulsing shoulder, while Mavis, produced a monogrammed handkerchief from her purse. "Ashes to ashes, dust to dust," the reverend went on.

"Here now, love," Mavis whispered, her eyes glistening with empathy as she handed the handkerchief to Donna.

"Th-thank you," Donna managed between sobs, clutching the handkerchief like a drowning man offered a buoy.

Gemma averted her eyes, determined to rein in her emotions. A chaffinch hopped along a nearby tombstone, tilting its head as if curious about the incomprehensible human drama that was unfolding before its eyes. Gemma found herself momentarily distracted by the feisty bird. Its brazenness was admirable.

Once the burial service concluded and the last amen echoed in the air, the mourners drifted away, their conversations a mix of bittersweet reminiscences and subdued farewells. The groundsman began refilling the grave in respectful silence, his spade slicing through the soil with rhythmic precision.

"Gemma, Mavis, would you join us at the wake?" Donna asked, her voice still tremulous, but steadier than before. She tucked a stray lock of hair behind her ear, an attempt to regain some semblance of composure. "It's at The Swan."

"Of course," Gemma replied, exchanging a look with Mavis. "We'd be delighted."

"Good, good. There's something I want to tell you."

Gemma felt surprised. What could Donna have to say *to them*? Why, she barely knew them! A glance at Mavis confirmed she was as confused as herself.

"Let's head off, shall we?" Gemma suggested, linking arms with both women.

Together, they walked toward the exit, past the ancient chapel with its watchful spire, leaving the chirping chaffinch behind.

Chapter Nine

Gemma meandered through the crowd of friends and acquaintances gathered in The Swan's function room. Glasses tinkled amid subdued conversations. Mavis, her hair impeccably set, walked by her side, surveying the buffet with a nod of approval.

"They've put on a nice spread, haven't they?" Her voice was appreciative, yet tinged with melancholy. Her mind kept going back to her dear Fred's wake. *For all his faults*, Mavis thought, *Dominic seemed well-liked by the community*. His wake was a well-populated affair.

"Indeed," Gemma said, her gaze drifting over the selection of finger sandwiches and scones. But she had lost her appetite.

Their attention shifted as Donna emerged from a cluster of mourners. The three of them had come to The

Swan together, but the moment they entered, Donna had been swept away by people eager to pay their tributes to her late husband. As it was, Gemma could barely contain her curiosity.

Seeing Donna extricate herself from the crowd, Mavis elbowed Gemma gently. As they approached, Donna caught sight of them and managed a wistful smile.

"Let's find somewhere quieter to sit," Donna suggested, her eyes scanning for an escape from the gentle murmur of condolences.

The trio settled themselves at a corner table, away from the crowd. Gemma leaned in, "Are you alright, Donna?" she asked earnestly.

Donna's lips twitched into a half-smile, but her eyes betrayed unease. "Something's bothering me," she confessed. She glanced between Gemma and Mavis, as if uncertain how much she should reveal.

Gemma's curiosity was piqued further. "What's that?"

"You can tell us, my dear, it's okay," Mavis urged, gently patting Donna's arm.

Donna exhaled slowly. "I heard from the pathologist when they released the body. It appears that Dominic died from an overdose of propranolol — the beta blockers he was taking for his heart problem." She paused. "But it just doesn't make any sense."

A chill ran through Gemma despite the warmth of

the room. "An overdose? How come?" She shared a puzzled look with Mavis.

"Why would Dominic take an overdose? Was he depressed?"

"Not that I know of. He was meticulous with his medication. Set a timer on his phone so he'd never forget to take it."

"Could he have stopped taking it? You know, to hoard the tablets?" Mavis interjected.

"Unlikely. The pathologist mentioned that a significant quantity of the medication was found in his system. If he'd stopped for that long, there would've been other health issues much earlier."

"Then perhaps he took fewer doses — every other day or so? Saved them up?"

"Even then," Donna cut in, "that amount would require months of hoarding."

"And if he wanted to end things..." Gemma began, "Well, I can't help but think that there are more straightforward ways than taking an overdose of his prescription medication."

"Yes, that's true," Mavis said, her voice barely above a whisper. "He could've used sleeping pills, or something else over-the-counter. No need for such a convoluted plan."

"Besides," Gemma added, disbelief colouring her words, "if he were suicidal, why agree to a book reading at the shop? And why take the overdose *right before* a public event? It just doesn't seem to fit. He had everything to live for. A successful book, money, fame, you name it. And even a reconciliation with you, Donna!"

They sat in silence for a moment. The soft hum of hushed conversations around them did nothing to ease the tension between the trio. Mavis leaned forward.

"Can't one simply order this medicine online? You can get anything online these days," she whispered. "Perhaps he took it to make his passing seem accidental?"

Donna shook her head, The Swan's antiquated chandelier casting ominous shadows across her face. "No, you need a prescription for that. An online pharmacist wouldn't dispense it otherwise."

Gemma watched Donna — the subtle quiver of her lips, the way her hand trembled ever so slightly. She seemed to be gathering the resolve to say something.

"I have a theory," Donna confessed after a brief pause. She glanced over her shoulder before continuing. "But sadly, I have no proof."

Gemma's heart raced. She sensed the gravity of what was to come. "At least you can tell us."

"Ellie," Donna hissed out the name as if it left a bitter taste in her mouth. "Dominic said he ended things with her recently. What if— what if she wanted revenge?"

Shock rippled through Gemma, followed swiftly by disbelief. She exchanged a wide-eyed glance with Mavis, whose mouth was agape. "I understand your position, really. But you can't just fling accusations around like that," Gemma whispered. "Especially not here at the funeral."

"I know," Donna whispered, her voice barely audible above the soft clink of glasses and murmur of voices around them. There were tears in her eyes. "I know."

"But if you say something about Ellie..." she hesitated, her eyes widening in horror as the implication of her own words settled over her. "Then you're putting yourself in the hot seat as well," Gemma finished. "You had your reasons to be upset with Dominic, given his... actions."

Donna's hand flew to her mouth, muffling a gasp. "Oh! I hadn't even thought of that."

"Precisely why, if you suspect Ellie, you need to tread carefully, my dear," Mavis said, ever the voice of pragmatic caution. "Your own story must be as clear as crystal."

Gemma rolled her eyes at the suggestion, not for its wisdom, but for the insinuation behind it. "Mavis, that sounds remarkably like tampering. We mustn't entertain such talk."

"Tampering?" Donna echoed, her voice a fragile thread in the quiet room. She fixed Gemma with a look of shock and vulnerability. "Do you— do you think *I* did it?"

"I didn't say that," Gemma replied. "I'm saying that

if the police suspect foul play, they will question everyone, won't they? Including you. It's standard procedure."

Donna's pallor deepened. She clutched at the edge of the table, as though hoping it might anchor her to reality. "What makes you think that? Why would they question me? Dominic and I were about to get back together, after all!"

"Because I've had a front-row seat to the sleuthing process before." Gemma recalled past conversations that felt all too relevant now. "My ex-fiancé is a detective. Their mantra was "Assume nothing, believe no one, and check everything." ABC, they called it — the fundamental principles of serious investigation."

"Sounds very Poirot to me," Mavis murmured. There was a note of grudging admiration in her voice as she imagined detectives sifting through threads of truth and lies, piecing together intricate puzzles.

"Perhaps," Gemma conceded with a soft sigh, watching the worry lines deepen on Donna's forehead. "But it's thorough."

Donna's finger traced around the rim of her glass. "I just don't know what to do," she murmured, more to herself than to the others.

Gemma reached out and put her hand on Donna's shoulder. "Donna, you need to take a step back, think everything through, and choose your words carefully.

Accusations of murder are serious business, especially with no proof."

Donna nodded. Her gaze searched the patterned tablecloth, as if the answers she sought rested in its fabric. "I will," she promised, though her tone suggested that her questions outnumbered answers.

"Have you ever met Ellie?" Gemma asked. More than anything, she felt curious about the relationships between these people, the tangled mess Dominic had left in his wake. Had this very tangle led to his untimely death?

"Once," Donna confessed. "She seemed quite nice, which feels like a pathetic thing to say about the woman who's sleeping with your husband." A bitter chuckle escaped her lips. "But I don't know if Dominic was with her before or after we split. I know there was someone else in the fray at some point, but Ellie... I'm not sure if we overlapped."

"Well, that's an important detail, isn't it?" Mavis had been listening intently. Now she chimed in matter-of-factly. "If Ellie only came into the picture after you two split, then technically, she hasn't done anything wrong, you know. I mean, in terms of philandering with a married man."

"Technically," Donna agreed, "but it's the visible ones you remember, isn't it? The others fade into the background." Her voice was hollow.

"Appearances can be very deceptive," Gemma

offered, thinking of the countless books she'd read where the most obvious suspect was seldom the culprit. There were always a few red herrings. She wondered, not for the first time, if life was imitating the mysteries that lined the shelves of the Bookworm.

Donna's gaze drifted absently over the array of sandwiches and sausage rolls. "I just don't know when Dominic started seeing Ellie," she said, her fingers tearing a napkin to pieces. She was desperately trying to make some sense of the tangled threads in her own mind. "Ellie was just so... visible."

"Her visibility makes sense, Donna," Gemma said, choosing her words carefully. "After you'd split, Dominic wouldn't have needed to sneak around. Anyone he was with before would've been his little secret. Look, I know this is hard, but don't be rash. Accusing Ellie of attempting to poison Dominic — that's serious. That's really serious, Donna. You can't accuse someone based on a hunch alone. You need evidence, and a compelling motive, of which you have neither." Gemma paused. "If you suspect that this wasn't an overdose, you need to inform the police to begin with. The only thing accusing Ellie would accomplish would be to make *you* look spiteful. Let the police investigate."

Donna nodded. The fight had drained out of her. "You're right, I suppose. I won't say anything about Ellie to anyone." She gave a defeated sigh.

"They said it was 'death by self-poisoning with propranolol.' Does that mean they aren't looking any further?" She said, almost as an afterthought.

"I honestly don't know," Gemma replied. "But if there *has* been foul play, the police will need to know. You'll need more than an accusation or a theory, though. Give it a little time. Today has been extremely traumatic for you." She took Donna's hand in hers. "Go home and get some rest. Do anything that keeps your mind off this. And remember, you can call me any time you want to talk."

"Thank you." Donna murmured, managing a weak smile.

A lull in their conversation allowed Gemma's attention to wander back to the teenage boy they had seen earlier.

"That teenage boy we saw earlier," Gemma mused, "the one at the funeral — do you have any idea who he might be?"

Donna shook her head. "No clue. I couldn't even see his face properly. Probably just a local kid being nosy...or curious."

"Probably," Gemma murmured. "But why conceal himself? I can understand Ellie skulking away and keeping a distance. But him? It just seemed odd."

Gemma shifted in her seat, smoothing her black dress as she tried to refocus on the present. She glanced at the small clock above the bar. Time was ticking away.

With a slight nod at Mavis, she steered the topic away from the morbid and toward the mundane.

"I might try the quiche," she said to Mavis, pointing to the buffet table. "It's got a lovely crust."

Mavis smiled. "Yes, that sounds lovely!" she said with a twinkle in her eye. "And oh, the spinach and feta one looks divine."

Donna accepted the change of subject. "I'll never understand how they get the pastry so flaky." Her voice was still weary, but lighter now.

"Must be all the butter," Gemma said, eliciting a chuckle from both women. The mood at their little table lifted, even if only for a moment. They rose to mingle with the other guests, who were also trying to navigate the sombre occasion with polite small talk and subdued laughter.

As Gemma wove her way through the crowd, she couldn't help but let her gaze wander around the room. Her eyes scanned the faces present, some familiar, others strangers. After Donna's allegations, Gemma's curiosity was piqued. She had a lot of questions about the woman whose absence was as conspicuous as the untouched cucumber sandwiches.

"It's a shame that Ellie isn't here," she murmured to Mavis while they waited in line at the buffet table.

"I'm sure she wouldn't be welcome, but it must be hard on her not to attend," Mavis said, reaching for a piece of quiche. “It would be interesting to speak to her. You know, to see how she’s doing.”

“Is that a hint of Miss Marple showing there, Mavis?”

“Who, me?" Mavis smiled. "Oh, I’m a little more modern than Miss Marple, my dear. Jessica Fletcher, maybe.”

Gemma couldn’t help but imagine a plot twist where the missing mourner played a pivotal role. She filed the thought away under ‘*further investigation*’.

For now, she put the theories on the back-burner, opting instead to refill her plate and continue the wake in true English fashion — by discussing the unpredictable weather, and the promising blooms in Mrs Colchester’s garden. It wasn’t time for sleuthing. Yet.

Chapter Ten

The next day, it was business as usual. Stationed behind the counter, Gemma slid an illustrated all-in-one edition of *Lord of the Rings* across to an eager customer, who looked giddy with anticipation at a journey into Middle-Earth.

"Isn't it a treasure?" Her fingers lingered on the book's ornate cover. "And these new illustrations bring Tolkien's world *so vividly* to life."

"Absolutely!" the customer exclaimed, cradling the book as if it were the most precious ring in the Shire. "I can't wait to get lost in its world again this weekend. Haven't read it since I was a kid!"

"Enjoy!" Gemma said with a genuine smile, watching as the customer exited. Nothing made her happier than watching someone barely able to contain their excitement about reading the book they bought.

As the usual hum of the store settled around her, Gemma couldn't shake off yesterday's exchange. Donna's allegations of Ellie deliberately poisoning Dominic. Of his death not being an accidental overdose... all these echoed in her head, casting a shadow over the peaceful morning.

Mavis, straightening a stack of Richard Osman novels nearby, caught Gemma's eye. Her usually cheerful face bore an expression of grave concern.

"Have you thought about what Donna said?" Gemma whispered. Sarah was bustling about with trays of tea and scones for the customers.

"Yes, I have, dear. A lot. And it doesn't sit right with me at all." Mavis shook her head, her brows furrowed.

"Nor with me," Gemma said, pursing her lips. "But it's not wise to discuss it here." She looked again at Sarah, who was balancing cups on a tray while chatting with a regular.

Mavis's eyes sparkled. "Why don't you come over to my house this evening? We can talk things through then, we'll have all the privacy we need."

Gemma considered the offer with a mix of excitement and trepidation. Were they actually going to delve deeper into this mystery? "That sounds perfect, Mavis."

"Excellent! We'll conduct our own investigation — just like in one of these murder mysteries!" Mavis gestured to the books she'd been arranging.

"Exactly," Gemma beamed, her spirits lifted by

Mavis's enthusiasm. Who'd have thought they'd get to unravel an actual puzzle — a murder mystery, no less — in sleepy little Belper?

Mavis leaned in. "I have a large dining room at home that's barely used now. We can spread out some rolls of paper on the wall and jot everything down. Like mapping out a treasure hunt!" Her eyes lit up with excitement.

"Sounds like something straight out of Sherlock Holmes!" Gemma chuckled, picturing herself in a tweed cap, magnifying glass in hand. The thought was oddly exhilarating.

"It does, rather! And I've been mulling over a few theories myself," Mavis confided, tapping a finger against her temple. "But we'll need to be very quiet about all of it. At least until we've got something concrete to show."

Gemma nodded. She was picturing their makeshift war room. Papers filled with hurriedly jotted theories strewn on Mavis's dining table, pictures pinned on the walls with diagrams scrawled with markers — you know, the way they did in those American detective shows. And most importantly, a chance to finally make a *real* change, to actually help the cause of justice, not just read about it! She could barely contain her excitement.

The sound of Sarah's footsteps interrupted these reveries. "Going on my break now, Gemma," she called. The morning rush had died down.

"That's fine," Gemma replied. As the door shut behind Sarah, Mavis and Gemma exchanged a quick, knowing glance. The thrill of their clandestine plan was clearly visible on their faces.

"We should really sit down and sift out everything we know up until now. See if there's even a case, you know..." Gemma mused.

"Indeed," Mavis said. "But what happens if we stumble across something— incriminating?"

Gemma considered this for a few moments. She had practically grown up between the pages of detective novels. She revelled in the twists and turns, the ins and outs of fictional crime investigation. And she was never one to shy away from an intricate puzzle, or a juicy murder mystery. But this wasn't a fun beach read. This was real life, with real people and real consequences.

"If it comes to that," Gemma said firmly, "I'll have to contact the police. Maybe talk to Dave. The police would need to be involved if we uncover anything concrete."

Mavis's eyes narrowed. "You're right, of course. Let's just hope it doesn't come to that."

"Yes, let's hope so," Gemma sighed. "The prospect of talking to my ex about something that ruined our relationship in the first place is not what I would call *ideal*."

Chapter Eleven

Mavis opened the door with a welcoming smile. Gemma stepped into the hallway, curious and excited. "Mavis, your house is delightful!" she exclaimed, taking in the neat, spacious drawing room. There was a cosy Chesterfield sofa on one side of the room, flanked by a little Victorian side-table, topped with a bowl of violets. A stone fireplace adorned the other corner, the marble mantelpiece strewn with old, grainy photos. Light poured in from the large French windows behind the sofa.

"Thank you, my dear," Mavis smiled. "It's far too big for only me now. But I just can't bear to part with it." She ushered Gemma through to the kitchen, a homely room with weather-beaten stone walls. Copper pots hung above the sizeable island, and herbs lined the windowsill.

"Can I get you something to drink? Coffee, perhaps?"

"A white coffee with no sugar, please," Gemma replied, settling onto a wooden stool by the worktop. She watched as Mavis quickly prepared their drinks, the kitchen filling with the rich, vibrant smell of coffee. Gemma also detected a scent of something sweet and buttery, and her eyes soon spied a stack of cherry flapjacks on a ceramic plate.

"Oh, those look delicious!"

"I made them when I got back from the shop," Mavis said with a smile. "I thought we'd need some sustenance for our sleuthing!"

Coffee mugs and flapjacks in hand, they made their way to the dining room. It was a picture of Victorian elegance, dominated by a large, carved mahogany table. A sideboard against one wall held a series of decorative plates, glasses, and a charming collection of porcelain teapots. But Gemma's eye was fixed on one slightly unusual addition to the décor — a piece of old wallpaper was taped to one wall, the decorative side facing the wall.

"Got the idea to create our very own murder board," Mavis chuckled. "Popped into the stationery shop earlier and got us some sticky notes and marker pens, too." She swept an arm towards the makeshift board, as if unveiling a modern art masterpiece.

Gemma laughed, the corners of her eyes crinkling up with delight. "You've turned your dining room into the set of a crime drama, Mavis. I feel like detectives will burst through the door any minute now!"

"Only the best for our investigation," Mavis beamed mischievously, setting down their drinks and distributing the flapjacks. Gemma was suddenly struck by the delight and playfulness that pervaded their demeanour. The task they were going to undertake was no child's play — it was serious, grave, even terribly dangerous.

But Gemma didn't really believe it would be serious. After all, they were simply investigating Donna's allegations, not the 'case'. There really was nothing to suggest foul play in Dominic's death, or the police would have caught up on it by now. So surely, there could be no harm in making an evening out of tackling this little 'mystery' that had knocked at their doorstep. Right?

While Gemma ruminated on this grave incident in their quiet little town, Mavis uncapped a black marker pen and approached the hanging wallpaper. With a flourish, she wrote "Dominic" in capital letters in the middle and circled it.

"So, what do we know so far?" she asked, stepping back to examine her handiwork. The uncapped marker tapped against her chin.

"Next to nothing, actually. But we can start with Ellie. She's at the heart of the accusations," Gemma said, stirring her coffee absentmindedly. Mavis nodded.

"Can't discount Donna either," she added, scribbling both Ellie and Donna's names on the paper, anchoring them with lines to Dominic's central circle. Her handwriting was a curious mixture of flamboyant loops and spidery slants.

"True," said Gemma, sipping her coffee. It was warm and comforting. "But I think we should start with Ellie, since we know practically nothing about her."

"Go on." Mavis capped her pen and sat down.

"Ellie was involved with Dominic, but the timeline's hazy. Did their fling kick off post-Donna, or did it start during their marriage? And let's not forget Dominic was the one who ended things with Ellie. That's got to sting, right?"

"Potential motive, if ever there was one," Mavis murmured, almost to herself. She uncapped the pen again, and made a note near Ellie's name.

"Exactly." Gemma leaned forward. "Jilted lover, broken heart – classic ingredients for revenge."

Mavis arched an eyebrow, her gaze settling on the name 'Ellie'. "But is that enough to push someone over the edge? I mean, chances are, Ellie knew what she was in for. Dominic apparently had a bit of a reputation."

"Yes, seems a bit thin, doesn't it?" Gemma ran her finger on the rim of her coffee cup. "But then again, we don't know the full story there. There could be more under the surface." She paused. "We need to find out more about this Ellie. Her full name, for starters."

"Agreed," Mavis said. She quickly scribbled beneath Ellie's name: *'Motive: Being discarded'*. Then she paused thoughtfully, and slowly added a question mark at the end. They must give Ellie the benefit of doubt at this stage. She then shifted her weight, as if moving the conversation along with her body. "Let's move on to Donna."

Gemma nodded. "Donna was quick to pin the blame on Ellie. A bit *too* quick, maybe? It makes me wonder..." Her voice trailed off. "Could she be using misdirection to her advantage?"

"Possibly," Mavis conceded, tapping the pen against her chin. "Although... if she were guilty, surely she'd only be too glad that the death was ruled a suicide? Staying quiet would be the better strategy, instead of digging up dirt and risking a police investigation."

"Unless Donna's not clever enough to think things through," Gemma interjected. "We hardly know her, after all." Memories of Donna's words floated back to her — claims of reconciliation and a rekindled romance with Dominic. They had only her word, even for the fact that she was moving back in with him. How could they corroborate such a tale? It rested solely on Donna's testimony, as unsubstantial as fog. "We need proof, Mavis. Something, *anything* concrete."

Mavis was already scribbling away under Donna's name. "There's the split," Gemma pointed out after a pause of deliberation. "Donna and Dominic parted ways nine months ago."

"True," Mavis muttered without looking up. She

drew a rough timeline onto the paper. "But if vengeance was her plan, why uncork it now? She could've done it immediately after the split too."

"My thoughts exactly," Gemma affirmed. "Why wait? What could have happened to trigger these actions *now*?" They shared a knowing look. They must first understand Donna, and the dynamics of her marriage with Dominic.

Mavis changed tack. "Right, let's dissect this overdose." She drew a line from Dominic's name, and looped it around a hastily written '*poisoning*' labelled with the drug '*propranolol*'. Above it, she inscribed the pressing question: '*How did the killer get the medication? How and when did Dominic ingest it?*'

"Propranolol, of all things," Gemma mused, sipping her coffee. "It's not your run-of-the-mill headache tablet. It's prescribed, controlled. Why choose that? Unless..."

"Unless it was meant to reinforce that only Dominic could've had access to it," Mavis concluded. "A more common drug might've raised immediate suspicions. The police *would* do a routine inquiry had it been another over-the-counter drug. But this — it smacks of a personal touch."

"Exactly," Gemma said with a nod. "A cunning ploy to make the suicide theory stick like treacle. After all, what could appear more natural than Dominic taking one too many pills, either by accident or design?"

Mavis set the pen down. She took a deep breath and scanned the writing on the wall. Gemma couldn't help but smile. Mavis looked every bit the lady detective, her brow furrowed and her eyes fixed on the board with a burning intensity. Jessica Fletcher would've been proud.

"But if he'd taken an entire bottle of paracetamol, or something of that ilk, it would scream suicide too, wouldn't it?" Mavis pondered aloud, her head tilting to one side.

"True," Gemma conceded. She bit her lip. "But Mavis, it just doesn't fit. Dominic was at the reading with us. He seemed excited to be there. He looked pale, yes. But even so, he didn't strike me as a man planning to do away with himself." She bit into a flapjack to give herself time to think.

Mavis nodded pensively, her pen tapping out a silent rhythm on the edge of the table. "That's what puzzles me too, my dear. If he meant to overdose, why not seclude himself? Why do it right before coming to a public event? No, someone *wanted* it to look like an accident." She scrawled the words '*murder?*' on the paper, underlined twice for emphasis.

"Someone with a grudge, or something to gain, maybe," Gemma murmured, the cogs turning in her mind.

"He was quite chipper when I saw him last week. Not the demeanour of a man done with life or wallowing in despair."

"I think we need to dig around Donna and Ellie more. Find out if they have alibis, see if they have motives," Gemma proposed.

"Absolutely! We know Donna's full name, so that could be our starting point."

"Right. Let's see where these names lead us."

Gemma took her phone out of her pocket, and her fingers danced across the screen. The familiar blue and white interface of Facebook greeted her. She quickly typed 'Donna Westley' in the search bar. A profile popped up, revealing nothing more than a name and a smiling face in the photograph. The other details were private.

"Shall I add her as a friend?" Gemma asked. She already knew the answer, but still felt doubtful. Would it look bad, or too forward?

Mavis, who'd been sipping her coffee, placed the mug down with a decisive clink. "Absolutely," she encouraged, her voice rich with the thrill of their investigation. "You're just being friendly, after all."

With a nod, Gemma tapped on 'Add Friend', and leaned back in her chair, releasing a breath she didn't realise she'd been holding. "And now we wait for Donna to accept," she said, deliberately casual.

To pass the time, they each took up another piece of cherry flapjack from the plate. Gemma couldn't help but sigh with contentment. "These really are divine,

Mavis. We should consider adding them to the café menu!"

"Thank you, my dear," Mavis beamed. "Family recipe. They were Fred's favourite too."

The wait was brief. At a ping of a notification, Gemma's heart skipped a beat. She clicked open her phone to find that Donna had accepted her friend-request. Her once restricted Facebook profile was now an open book. Gemma and Mavis scrolled through it, as far back as they could go.

"Ah, look at this! Donna runs a business called 'Ultimate Business Coaching Ltd.'"

Mavis, ever the note-taker, scribbled the information on their 'murder board', her hurried letters more spidery than ever.

"A business owner. Interesting," Gemma mused, contemplating the layers this new information added to Donna's character. "We can check that out." Her gaze drifted further down the page. "She lives in Nottingham. That's probably where she moved after the split."

"Nottingham, eh? Quite the move," Mavis remarked, her hand hovering over the board.

"Indeed," Gemma said, her mind already spinning with possibilities. She scrolled further down, her eyes darting across the glowing screen. A new post appeared, showing a montage of smiling women with their arms linked, posing in front of the ancient walls of York — on the day before Dominic had met his untimely end.

"Mavis, look at this! Could this be an alibi?" Gemma suggested, her brows scrunched together in thought. "We should verify this."

"Oh yes, indeed." Mavis's words were half-swallowed by a yawn that she tried hard to stifle with a delicate palm. The excitement of their sleuthing endeavours remained unabated, but her body was giving way.

"Maybe we should call it a night, Mavis," Gemma smiled, noticing the fatigue on her friend's face.

"Perhaps just a few more minutes?" Mavis said, but another tell-tale yawn betrayed her.

"Tomorrow is another day," Gemma reminded her, putting her phone back in her pocket. "I'll need to get closer to Donna, see if she's really the grieving wife, or something more sinister. I'll think of ways to get on with it by tomorrow."

"Good plan." Mavis's voice was now a whisper of concurrence. "And don't forget about Ellie. We still need to figure out how to approach her."

"Absolutely." Gemma mapped out their next steps. "Tomorrow, we'll do some digging into Donna's business — public records will definitely reveal more than her Facebook profile does."

"We're doing quite the detective work, aren't we?"

"Elementary, my dear Mavis." Gemma gave a light chuckle.

She had come to appreciate this growing camaraderie between herself and Mavis. With a plan brewing and their knowledge growing deeper, Gemma felt a surge of anticipation for what was to come. Who knew what they might uncover next?

The clock on the wall chimed ten and Gemma stood up, stretching her arms above her head. She glanced at Mavis, whose eyes were filled with a mixture of excitement and exhaustion. "I'll see you in the morning. I'll give Donna a ring tomorrow, see how she's holding up. Maybe suggest we meet for a cuppa."

"This is all rather thrilling, isn't it?" Mavis grinned, a note of awe in her voice.

"It really is! We might not have a deerstalker or a magnifying glass, but we have sticky notes and determination. And flapjacks!" Gemma laughed, gathering her belongings.

She felt a surge of energy at the thought of the day ahead. This mystery beckoned her like a siren's call. With one last reassuring grin, Gemma stepped out into the cool night, the scent of cherry flapjacks lingering behind her.

Chapter Twelve

The next morning was a pleasant, albeit slightly cloudy one. The sunny spring seemed to have begun planning its exit. But the marketplace bustled with people as always, none the worse for some stray clouds. Gemma flipped the sign to 'Open', and stepped back into the familiar embrace of the Bookworm. Mavis, perched on a stool behind the counter, was staring intently through a crossword puzzle.

"I've got some news, but I'll share it at lunchtime," Gemma said.

Mavis's head snapped up, her crossword immediately forgotten. "Interesting news, you say? Does it have to do with our little mystery?"

"Perhaps," Gemma teased, her lips curving into a smile. "Let's just say it adds another layer to Donna's potential motive."

"Ooh, I can't wait!" Mavis clapped her hands, her eyes lighting up at the prospect of an intrigue.

But before she could prod further, the chime above the door announced the arrival of a delivery man, burdened with a large, square box. Gemma signed for the package, and hauled it gingerly onto the counter.

"Whatever could that be?" Mavis asked with undisguised curiosity, craning her neck to get a better look as Gemma sliced through the tape with a letter opener.

"Ah, it's the future — or so they tell me." Gemma lifted the cardboard flaps to reveal a neat stack of e-reader devices.

"Electronic books? Here?" Mavis's voice rose an octave. The Bookworm offering these new-fangled electronic devices? Sheer sacrilege! To Mavis, they might as well have been alien artefacts. "But we deal with proper books, Gemma! The kind you can hold and smell and—"

"I know, I know," Gemma interrupted this impassioned flow. She patted Mavis's hand soothingly. "But times are changing, and we need to offer folks a choice. Consider it an experiment."

"An experiment?" Mavis repeated, still wide-eyed and incredulous.

"Exactly. And I'm thinking of offering a setup service for anyone who buys one," Gemma continued. "You know, help them download their first book, show them how it all works. Could be a nice little earner, and we'd be keeping up with the youngsters too. Bring more of them through the doors!"

"Helping people with technology, eh?" Mavis considered this, rubbing her chin. Finally, she said in a tone of grudging acceptance, "Well, if anyone can make it seem less frightful, it's you, Gemma."

"Flattery will get you everywhere," Gemma replied, already picturing the rows of e-readers sitting alongside the leather-bound classics. "And I was thinking, Mavis, we could invest in high-quality second-hand books too — collectors' items and first editions, you know. The sort of books you'd want to display on your shelves at home."

"Now that could be a good business angle," said Mavis. "Collectible books that you couldn't replace with one of these e-book thingies. It will definitely help sales!"

At that moment, the ever-faithful bell heralded the arrival of another visitor — a bespectacled gentleman with a thoughtful frown, and a trimmed beard. He approached the counter, smoothing the lapel of his jacket.

"Good morning," he said, offering Gemma a polite nod. "I'm here on behalf of the St. Mary's Chess Club. We're in a bit of a pickle. Our usual venue has double-booked us with a rather raucous knitting circle."

Gemma was busy arranging the e-readers in a display that she hoped would entice even the most techno-phobic of her regulars. She looked up. "Ah, that sounds like an unfortunate mix-up," she replied, with a sympathetic tilt of her head.

"It is, indeed. It disrupted our plans at the very last minute, as it were. I saw your leaflet in the supermarket, about hiring the bookstore as a venue," he said. "We'd very much like to rent your store for our weekly gatherings. Every Thursday, from seven thirty to nine thirty in the evening. Space for ten tables. And of course, we'd buy refreshments from your café."

"Chess club, you say?" Gemma brightened at the idea. "I used to play a bit of chess myself, back in the day." She leaned closer to him as she added in a conspiratorial whisper, "Used to give the boys quite the run for their money."

The man smiled with a faint amusement. "Well then, we'd be honoured if you'd grace us with your presence. Perhaps even join in a game or two!"

"Let's settle on £30 an evening, shall we?" Gemma smiled, extending her hand.

"Most agreeable," the man replied with a firm handshake. "That is much more affordable than our current arrangement. And of course, with the bonus of tea and scones within arm's reach!"

"That's settled, then," Gemma smiled, picturing her shop filled with chess enthusiasts murmuring over their moves, the smell of fresh pastry mingling with the cerebral silence. The Bookworm would come alive, indeed.

As the chess enthusiast took his leave, Sarah peeked

out from the café. "All quiet on the western front, Gemma. I'll nip out for my break, if that's alright? Can you cover if any customers come in?"

"You got it, Sarah. Enjoy your break!"

Now alone with Mavis, who was straightening a shelf of reference books, Gemma decided it was time to confer. "Mavis, about Donna's motive," she began, placing her palms on the counter. Her tone dropped to convey the gravity of her discovery.

Mavis extricated herself from the encyclopaedias and joined her. "Go on."

Gemma pulled out a stack of printed papers from beneath the counter. "Last night, I did some digging into Donna's coaching business. It's a limited liability company, so her accounts are a matter of public record. The finances don't look good. Deep in debt, revenue plummeting. It's dire."

Mavis's eyebrows rose, almost touching her hairline. "Could that be why she was so keen to patch things up with Dominic? A little financial security, perhaps, what with all his literary success?"

"Or motivation for something more sinister," Gemma said, her eyes narrowing. "They were still married, so she'd be entitled to a chunk of his estate."

"Only if there's a will," Mavis pointed out. "Otherwise, she might have to share with his family."

"Either way, it puts money in her pocket." Gemma folded the papers, tapping them against the counter.

"Time to call Donna, see how she's faring — and maybe arrange a meet up."

"Be subtle, my dear," Mavis cautioned. "Keep her on our side."

"Subtlety is my middle name," Gemma said. She retreated to the privacy of the back room to make the call, leaving Mavis to mind the store.

Five minutes later, Gemma re-emerged. Mavis glanced up from the cash register, where she was handing a receipt to old Mrs Pemberton, who clutched a newly purchased gardening manual to her chest like a prized trophy.

"Everything all right?" Mavis whispered, careful not to draw their patron's attention.

"I spoke to Donna," Gemma announced, the moment Mrs Pemberton tottered out into the market-place. "I'm meeting her tomorrow. She wants to visit Dominic's house, but doesn't fancy going all alone."

"Understandable, given the circumstances." Mavis considered it. "You could glean more from her there — a change of environment might loosen her tongue."

"Maybe." Gemma chewed on her lip. It would require great conversational skills, and a truly delicate balance. "But I can't be too pushy. If Donna suspects we're digging, our new friendship will be over before it's even begun."

"Oh, don't worry, my dear," Mavis said. "You've got

the tact of a diplomat when you need it. Use that charm to keep her talking."

"Charm, eh?" Gemma smiled. "I'll add that to my detective toolkit."

"Make sure you do." Mavis gave her a firm nod.

Then, with an air of finality, she added, "Pop by mine tomorrow evening. We'll rifle through what you've found and separate the wheat from the chaff."

Chapter Thirteen

Gemma parked outside Dominic's house on Sandbed Lane, a quiet, tree-lined street at the north end of Belper. Donna was standing by the gate of what used to be her marital home.

"Thanks for swinging by, Gemma," said Donna. "It's just so— strange being here, you know? After everything."

"Of course," Gemma replied, offering a sympathetic smile. "I can't imagine how difficult this must be for you."

Donna gave a listless shrug. "I haven't set foot in this place since before we separated."

Gemma shifted her weight from one foot to the other, trying to find the right words to broach a delicate subject as they stood by the garden gate. The chirping of birds filled the tranquil air.

"Seems unfair, though, that you were the one to move out when Dominic was the one who..." she trailed off.

Donna's lips pressed into a thin line. "This house was Dominic's. Left to him by his parents." She glanced back at it, a tinge of resignation in her voice. "We didn't have any kids, you know. It just made sense that I should leave."

"Must've been a big change for you," Gemma remarked.

"Big is one word for it," Donna sighed. "I ended up in Nottingham, living with a friend who had a room to rent." Her tone was even, signalling a sort of listless acceptance of her situation.

"Shall we go in?"

"Yes, let's go."

Donna's hand was steady as she inserted the key in the lock and turned it. She pushed the door open and stepped inside, reaching for the alarm panel by the entrance and disabling it with a plastic fob attached to her keys.

"Always had a key, then?" Gemma ventured, following Donna over the threshold.

"Not since we split up, but he gave me the keys back recently, as we were moving back in together."

There was a pungent odour of bleach in the house.

They walked into the kitchen, which looked like something off the cover of a lifestyle magazine. The scent clawed at Gemma's throat, and she coughed into her sleeve. Donna's nose wrinkled in disgust. She strode to the kitchen window and thrust it open. A welcome rush of fresh air helped settle their senses.

"Blimey, did he take up cleaning as a hobby?" Gemma joked, though her brows were furrowed in concern.

"Not to this level no," Donna said. "He was never a messy person, to be sure. But this seems a bit excessive." She cast a questioning glance at the gleaming kitchen surfaces. "This is all new," she mused, more to herself than to Gemma. "This extension wasn't here when I left. Dominic's had it built recently. He's been busy."

"Did he hire a cleaner?" Gemma prodded, her curiosity piqued as she peered into the bin — spotless, recently emptied.

"Hardly," Donna scoffed, a ghost of a smile on her lips. "Dominic would never pay for a cleaner. This must be Ellie's handiwork."

"Ellie?" Gemma sounded sceptical. "You think she's been here since his passing?"

"Has to be. She did live here with him, you know," Donna said with a sideways glance. "Although I would've expected her to have left by now, considering I was supposed to be moving back in."

Gemma looked at the kitchen, struck by how meticulously clean everything was. She paused by the cooker, noting the absence of the usual grease marks and stains.

She tried her best to sound casual. "Where did he keep his medication?"

"In the old kitchen, it was above the cooker. In a box," Donna recalled, moving towards the sleek new cooker. She opened the cupboard and took out a plain cardboard box.

Donna opened the box. Inside lay one and a half splinter packs of Dominic's medicine, Propranolol. She plucked them out, and held them up for Gemma to see.

"That's strange," Donna murmured. "If he overdosed on the amount mentioned in the pathologist's report, then there should be none left in this!"

"Definitely odd," Gemma agreed. Donna replaced the medicine box in the cupboard above the cooker. She picked up the kettle, filled it, set it on its base and flicked the switch. Then she opened the fridge, and inspected a carton of milk. A sniff confirmed its freshness.

"Tea or coffee?" Donna asked over her shoulder.

"Tea, please," Gemma replied, grateful for the offer.

Mugs clattered onto the counter as Donna busied herself with the ritual of tea-making.

Gemma, seeking to lighten the mood, ventured into safer waters. "I saw the photos of York on your Facebook," she said, her tone airy. "It's such a charming place. Those side streets resemble Diagon Alley from Harry Potter!"

"York is lovely!" Donna exclaimed, a small yet sincere smile breaking through. "We were there for a friend's birthday. Drove back the same day Dominic..." When she continued after a few moments, her voice had a steel edge. "We were at a service station on the way home when I found out about his death."

"Must've been an awful shock," Gemma said, watching as Donna's hands moved mechanically, squeezing the tea-bags against the sides of the mugs.

"It was..." Donna's voice cracked. "Ellie! She must have done this, and then scrubbed the kitchen clean — to within an inch of its life!" She handed Gemma a steaming, olive green mug. Her movements were brisk and jerky, as if she was desperately trying to outrun thoughts of the woman she blamed.

"Thank you," Gemma murmured, accepting the tea. She wrapped her fingers around the warmth of the mug, feeling the heat seep into her skin.

She took a couple of sips and then set her mug down with a slight clink against the black granite surface. "There isn't any concrete proof yet that Ellie committed the murder," she reiterated, carefully studying Donna's reaction.

Donna's grip on her mug tightened. "It must be her," she insisted, her voice thick with conviction. "Who else could it be?"

The question hung in the air, heavy and unanswerable.

"Does Dominic have cameras installed in the house?" Gemma asked. "Like one of those doorbell cameras. I didn't see anything on the front door."

"I suppose not. He never did before. He wasn't the fancy technology kind of person," Donna replied, stepping through the kitchen door into the hallway. "There are only alarm sensors on the wall. No cameras," she confirmed.

"Can you check the alarm log?"

"I wouldn't even know how."

"Let me look," said Gemma, stepping into the hallway. She tapped some commands on the control panel.

"We have a similar system in the shop," she explained. A series of log entries appeared on the small digital screen.

"I can see where we entered this morning. Your alarm fob is called 'Fob 2'," Gemma informed, going through the entries. "The last entry and exit were on the Wednesday, the day after Dominic died, at..." Gemma halted abruptly.

"What is it?" asked Donna.

"Someone came in the house at 3.30 in the morning and stayed until 5.35 am. They used Fob 3." Gemma's voice was thoughtful.

"The only person I can think of who'd have another alarm fob is Ellie," said Donna.

Gemma kept looking at the entries. "The previous entry was the Tuesday morning, about 9.15am with Fob

1. That must have been Dominic, as he left to do the reading at the store." She scrolled further through the past week of alarm logs. "They are all Fob 1, so we can safely say that that was Dominic."

"This is our evidence then! Ellie's the only person who could have Fob 3. We need to find out!" Donna sounded almost desperate. They walked back into the kitchen and perched on the barstools at the counter.

"That gives us a more solid lead, I must admit," Gemma said. "Does Ellie live around here?" Here curiosity was higher than ever. *What were the actual dynamics between these people?*

"Ellie lives in Belper," Donna said flatly. "Works at that coffee shop on King Street." She shrugged, her shoulders weighed down seemingly by resentment. "I never go in there, actually. But she lived here, in this house. So she definitely had access."

"Right," Gemma murmured, trying to take all this in. "And when did Dominic end things with her?"

"Before we decided to reconcile," Donna answered. She paused just long enough for Gemma to discern a flicker of doubt in her eyes. "That's what he told me."

"Why did you decide to give it another go, if you don't mind me asking?" Gemma braced herself for a rebuke. This *was* a bit too forward. She could almost hear Mavis's reproach of "Subtle!"

Donna's pause stretched out. Gemma sheepishly started, "I'm sorry, I shouldn't have—"

"No, it's fine," Donna cut in, her voice softer now. "I missed him. And he missed me. Said he was sorry for everything. He seemed genuinely remorseful."

Seemed, Gemma thought, her gaze flitting to the window. She wondered if there was more to Donna's willingness to reconcile than just missing Dominic. Did the failure of her business play a part? The thought lingered, but Gemma filed it away for now, choosing to sip her tea instead of stirring the pot further.

Donna walked hesitantly to the front door. Her hand hovered over a pile of envelopes and leaflets that had accumulated like fallen leaves inside the wire mesh mail cage. She gathered them up in a neat stack and returned to the kitchen.

"Is it even right for me to open these?" Donna asked, thumbing uncertainly through the post.

"Well, you *were* married to him," Gemma said soothingly. "Besides, dealing with his affairs is a part of the process."

With a small nod, as if granting herself permission, Donna selected a letter from the top of the pile. She sighed and held it up.

"Bank statement," she said, tearing open the envelope. "Oh, my gosh!"

It was a sudden cry. Gemma's eyes snapped up just in time to see Donna turn pale as she scanned the contents of the statement.

Chapter Fourteen

Gemma rushed to Donna's side. Whatever the bank statement said, Donna certainly hadn't expected it. She had turned white as a sheet and seemed utterly crushed, as if the very life had drained out of her. The numbers must have been dismal.

"Can you believe this? He's up to his eyebrows in debt. I thought he was doing well, Gemma! Dominic always had that air of someone who didn't need to check the price tag."

"Perhaps he was just good at keeping secrets," Gemma said, puzzled. "His book was quite the talk of the town, wasn't it? It flew off the shelves at my shop. Surely, the royalties..."

Donna's tired eyes lit up at that. She paced around the kitchen. "His first few royalty cheques were impressive. But I haven't seen any of his recent statements, of course." Then she paused, her resolve returning. With quick strides, she left the kitchen and headed towards the lounge.

Gemma followed, curiosity nipping at her heels. Donna reached Dominic's desk — an elaborate mahogany affair. She slid open a drawer and rifled through papers until her hand landed on a stack of envelopes. Each one was marked with the logo of the publishing house.

Back in the kitchen, Donna leafed through the royalty statements with a growing sense of dread. Gemma read over Donna's shoulder. The figures told a story of plummeting success. The initial three statements boasted hefty sums, but thereafter, the amounts had dwindled down into almost nothing.

"Looks like he's been living a king's life on a pauper's purse," Gemma mused.

Donna frowned. "And this new extension..." She gestured towards the new kitchen. "I don't even want to think about how much that cost."

"Do you think he could have squirrelled away some funds elsewhere? Savings, investments?" Gemma suggested.

Donna shook her head. "If he was in this much debt," she said, glancing around Dominic's kitchen that seemed more like a gilded cage now, "then I guess the house will need to be sold." Her voice caught on the word *sold*, as if she found the reality hard to swallow.

"Did he, by any chance, hint at any financial worries when you two talked about getting back together?"

"Not a whisper." Tears gathered in Donna's eyes. "He made it sound like everything was coming up roses."

The room grew quiet, except for the ticking of the wall clock. Then, as if struck by lightning, Donna gasped. "Wait! We're still married!" Her hand flew to her mouth. "Does this mean I'll be saddled with all his debts?"

"Oh no, not necessarily. I mean, only if they're in your name too," Gemma reassured her, though her knowledge of marital finance was limited. "If the debts are in his name alone, then legally, you shouldn't be responsible for them, surely. But they would need to be paid off from his estate."

Donna sank back into her chair. The fight drained out of her as quickly as it had arrived. "I didn't know things were this dire," she whispered.

A flush of anger rose in her cheeks. "Ellie... I always knew she was after his money!"

"Let's not jump to conclusions, Donna," Gemma said, even as her own mind ticked over the possibilities. "We don't have proof of that."

Donna shook her head, unwilling to even consider that Ellie could be innocent. Her shoulders dropped.

"You're right, of course," she finally conceded, becoming subdued with the admission. "Sorry, it's just... All of this is— is a bit much."

"Understandable," Gemma said. She reached across the table to give Donna's hand a brief, comforting squeeze. Donna spread the papers across the kitchen table.

"The last thing I need is more debt," she said, pinching the bridge of her nose. "My coaching business is already on its knees."

Gemma leaned in. "What do you mean?" Feigning ignorance to Donna's business woes.

"Ever since this cost-of-living crisis hit, people are holding back on spending," Donna explained, tracing a finger over the royalty statement figures that no longer added up in her favour. "They're cautious, and it's really hurting the business. I might have to shut it down before it gets any worse."

"Times are tough all around," Gemma said, thinking of her own cherished bookshop. "People can find books cheaper online these days. Even for free, sometimes. It's squeezing us little shops out." There was a moment of shared understanding as they looked at each other, two local businesswomen caught in the same whirlwind.

Gemma searched for a change of subject. "Do you think Dominic could have been depressed because of his debts?" She examined Donna closely. "Uncontrolled debt can really weigh on people, you know. Cause a lot of anxiety."

Donna shook her head. "I don't know about depression or anxiety. He didn't show any signs of it. When we spoke about giving things another go, he was... Well, he was Dominic. Full of himself, as usual."

"Could it have been suicide, then?" Gemma prodded. The question felt like poking a sleeping bear.

"Absolutely not." The fierce answer startled Gemma a little. "Dominic had his faults, but taking his own life? No!" Donna's eyes flashed with a conviction that bordered on defiance. "You... you don't understand. You didn't know him. He was too *arrogant* to just give up! There's foul play at work here, Gemma — I can feel it in my bones."

The sudden shrill ringing of the doorbell sliced through the tense air. Gemma watched as Donna, clearly confused, sprang to her feet and made her way to the front door. There was a brief, muffled exchange, and suddenly, Gemma heard raised voices.

"Excuse me! What do you think you are doing? Who are you?"

Gemma rose from her chair, and craned her neck to see past the archway. A man pushed his way past a flustered Donna and stormed into the kitchen.

"Can we help you?" Gemma asked, her tone calm despite her rapidly pounding heart. The stranger didn't even acknowledge her. His gaze was locked on Donna.

With her hands on her hips, Donna mirrored the man's scowl with one that could curdle milk. "Well?"

The unexpected visitor seemed momentarily lost for words, chest heaving as if he'd run a marathon to get here. Apparently, whatever news he bore was urgent enough to outweigh common courtesy.

Chapter Fifteen

"I'm Geoff Dunsworth."

He was a short, stocky man, with unkempt flaxen hair that he kept running grubby fingers through. His palms were rough like sandpaper, and his sallow, weather-beaten face was slowly turning beet-red. He glared at Donna, his eyes steely and unforgiving.

"Are you Donna?" he barked, and without waiting for an answer, he continued, "I'm the one who built this fancy kitchen and the blasted extension. And I'll tell you, it wasn't out of the kindness of my heart!"

Donna gripped the edge of the table for support. Gemma quickly positioned herself between the two of them, like a referee preparing to mediate a boxing match.

"Mr Dunsworth, let's just all take a breath here." She hastened to deescalate the situation. Her voice was firm, but not unkind.

Geoff huffed. His chest deflated, and he ran a calloused hand through his hair, making it stick up on all sides. "That husband of hers," he spat, jerking a thumb at Donna, "owes me thirty grand for the work I did. Thirty grand! Every time I asked him for payment, he fed me another story. 'The money is coming,' he'd say. But it never did. I don't want any empty promises now — I want my money!"

"Thirty grand..." Gemma echoed, stunned beyond words. She glanced at Donna, who had turned pale-white, and then turned back to Geoff.

"The money is coming! The money is coming!" Geoff performed a high-pitched imitation of Dominic. "More like excuses were coming. Now he's gone, and I'm left holding the bag!" He snorted derisively.

Gemma gently placed her hand on Donna's shoulder. This was a truly delicate puzzle to piece together, and Mr Dunsworth was, in jigsaw terms, shaped like a sledgehammer.

Geoff's face turned an even deeper shade of crimson, and the blue veins in his temple pulsed with fury. "Look, if I don't get that money, my business is finished! Do you understand that?" His forefinger jabbed at Donna. "You're his wife, aren't you? That means his debts are your problem now!"

Donna flinched. Her demeanour spelled sheer astonishment. Her eyes oscillated between shock, fear, and a righteous fury. Finally, they settled on fury.

"That's not how it works! We were separated, for heaven's sake! I didn't even know about this extension until recently!"

"Separated or not, that's none of my business," Geoff growled. "I did the work. I want my pay. And since Dominic isn't here to settle his account, it's on you, lady!"

"You can't just storm into someone's home and demand cash like that!" Donna yelled, her hands on her hips. "Where's your proof, anyway?"

With an exasperated grunt, Geoff dug into a worn leather bag that was slung over one shoulder. He fished out a stack of papers and slapped them onto the kitchen table. They were clearly invoices, with figures and dates underlined in thick, aggressive strokes. They fanned out all over the table, and fluttered in the spring breeze.

"Proof enough for you?" His eyes narrowed. "And because I'm not a total monster, I'll give you a week. One week, Donna. Get me my thirty grand!"

Gemma stood by the kitchen island, watching this drama unfold with an acute consciousness of her own awkward position. She'd prepared for an afternoon of sleuthing, of expertly guiding Donna into conversation in order to glean information and clues. Instead, she'd been dropped into the middle of a farcical play, except that the stakes were all too real. She felt compassion, and even a twinge of guilt, as she helplessly watched Donna trying to come to terms with the impossible dilemma that had been thrust upon her.

Tears brimmed in Donna's eyes. Her composure seemed to be cracking under the weight of Geoff's demands. Gemma stepped forth again.

"Look here, Mr Dunsworth," she began, her voice steady despite the apprehensions that clouded her mind. "Donna isn't familiar with any of this. She's only just begun to untangle Dominic's finances. It's going to take time to sort through the estate."

Geoff clenched his jaw, and his nostrils flared. He looked like a bull about to charge. "Not my problem!" he spat. "She ain't the only one with problems! I've got bills piling up, wages to pay, and mouths to feed!"

"Threatening a widow isn't the solution, Mr. Dunsworth. And it's not how we do things around here," Gemma answered with a polite iciness. "You'll get your money, I assure you. But intimidation?" She shook her head, allowing a moment for her words to sink in. "That's a story no one wants to read — especially not the police."

Geoff snorted. His eyes quickly flicked between the two women, as if sizing them up. Eventually, they landed on Gemma with a begrudging respect. He straightened up and prepared to leave, but not without having the last word. "One week, Donna. I won't let Dominic's mess ruin *me*. I've got a crew depending on me, and I'm not going to let them down!"

With that, he spun on his heel and stomped out of the kitchen. As the front door slammed behind him, Gemma let out a deep breath. Her heart was pounding, and questions assailed her mind, but she attempted to pull herself together. She wasn't the one in trouble here.

She turned to Donna, whose face was streaked with silent tears. The two of them stood there in absolute silence, broken only by the faint echo of the slammed door.

Donna's complexion had turned a deathly white. Her eyes darted desperately around the kitchen, as if searching for something to anchor herself to reality. In a voice so faint it could barely compete with the ticking of the wall clock, she murmured, "I didn't know any of this, Gemma. I didn't know about all this debt! Thirty thousand pounds! Oh, what am I going to do?"

Gemma sidled up to her friend. "First things first, we put the kettle on." She put on an encouraging smile, even as her own nerves were doing the foxtrot. "No problem was ever solved without a good cuppa."

The suggestion coaxed a weak smile from Donna, a temporary respite from the sheer panic that enveloped her features. Gemma bustled about the kitchen, filling the kettle.

"But a week, Gemma!" Donna whimpered, wrapping her arms around herself as if warding off a chill. "How can I possibly sort everything out in such a short time?"

"Geoff is just trying to intimidate you. After all, he needs the money just as much as you do. His bark is probably worse than his bite," Gemma reassured her.

But she herself wasn't so certain.

Chapter Sixteen

Gemma took in a deep breath as they finally walked out onto Sandbed Lane. Desolation and gloom clung to her like cobwebs after the uncomfortable kitchen encounter and the stifling emptiness of Dominic's house. She prayed that the crisp morning air would wash all her apprehensions away, and clear her mind.

Geoff's gruff voice still echoed in her head, his frustration palpable as he argued about outstanding payments for work on Dominic's house. She didn't want to think of what would transpire after his stipulated one week.

Donna strolled listlessly beside her, her shoulders slumped in defeat. "I can't believe I have to sell the house," she said, more to herself than to Gemma. "This was supposed to be our fresh start!" Her eyes brimmed with tears.

Walking down the lane, they saw Bill, Dominic's elderly neighbour, leaning against his front gate. Years of gardening under the sun had weathered his face, but his eyes sparkled with vitality. He had clearly lost none of his vigour.

"Morning, ladies," Bill greeted them with a nod. His eyes softened as they landed on Donna. "I'm so sorry for your loss." He doffed his cap, revealing a head of thinning hair, like the last leaves clinging to an autumn tree.

"Thank you, Bill," Donna replied, with a small but sincere smile. Bill had always been kind to her, even in the tumultuous times when she'd moved out. "He certainly left his mark on all of us."

"Indeed, he did," Bill agreed. "Can't quite believe he's gone. The place feels different without him."

Donna forced a polite smile. "Different, yes," she said, glancing back ruefully at her house.

"Are you okay, Donna?" His furrowed brows held genuine concern. "Are you still moving back in?"

"Trying to be," Donna sighed. "Just facing up to reality, is all. I don't really know about moving in at the moment."

Bill nodded. "If there's anything I can do, you just let me know. Don't hesitate."

"Thanks, Bill. That means a lot." Donna smiled.

Gemma took this opportunity to interject. "Bill,

have you noticed any unusual activity around here since Dominic... passed away?"

"Ah," Bill straightened up eagerly. He'd clearly been waiting for just such a question. "Now that you mention it, I did, yes. It was the morning after Dominic passed. I couldn't sleep properly, so I'd just made myself a nice cuppa and took it by the window. And then I saw a young man leaving your house. Early it was, about half five, just as the sun was peeking over the horizon."

Donna's eyebrows shot up. She gave Gemma a loaded glance.

Gemma's detective instincts kicked into full gear. "Did you recognise him?"

"Can't say I did, to be sure." Bill scratched his chin. "But he wasn't in a hurry or anything. Walked out calm as you like, and even locked the front door behind him. That's what struck me as a bit odd."

He shook his head, his expression a mix of curiosity and disbelief. "I couldn't see his face, though. He was wearing one of those large hoodies that all the youngsters seem to wear these days. Odd time for a visit, I said to myself. But he didn't strike me as a burglar. Like I said, he was too calm and just... normal. That's why I didn't raise an alarm."

"Strange indeed," Gemma said under her breath.

"Very," Donna agreed.

Bill leaned closer over the garden gate, the lines of

concern on his face deepening. “Does Dominic have a son or a nephew no one knows about?”

Donna’s face crumpled. “No. He doesn’t.”

“Strange,” Gemma mused, tucking a stray lock of hair behind her ear. “Because that sounds exactly like the boy I saw skulking around a tree during the funeral. He seemed out of place, just like this morning visitor. And he was also wearing a hoodie, do you remember?”

“Oh yes, I do. Odd, that. Do you think it’s the same person?”

“I don’t know. It seems like a strange coincidence.”

The conversation wound down awkwardly. Gemma offered a small, grateful smile to Bill. “Thank you, Bill. You’ve been more helpful than you know.”

“Anytime,” Bill replied with a gentle nod.

The two women turned away from the gate, their steps slowing down across the garden walkway as they processed this new information. When they reached the end of the walkway, Gemma turned to Donna.

“Donna, I can only imagine how difficult this is for you. Call me if you need anything, anything at all. Even just to talk.”

“I will do, thank you.” Donna gave her a small, grateful smile.

Gemma walked back to her own car. Slipping into the driver’s seat, she let out a deep sigh. Did this morning accomplish *anything*? She’d learned quite a lot — about Dominic, about Donna and their relationship.

The pieces of the puzzle were still scattered, but each new piece of information brought a potential edge or corner to light.

Gemma turned the key in the ignition. She paused for a few moments to determine what to do next, and quickly made a decision. She pulled away from the curb, taking a U-turn along Sandbed Lane.

Mavis lived nearby. She'd go to her house later and lay out all she had learned.

Chapter Seventeen

A customer approached the counter clutching a copy of the graphic novel *Batman: Year One*. Gemma gave him an encouraging smile.

"Fantastic choice! An exciting reimagining of the Batman origin story!" Her hands hovered over the cash register, a creature more temperamental than the English weather.

"Thanks!" the customer smiled, fishing out a crumpled ten-pound note from his pocket.

As Gemma rang in the sale, the cash box gave a mocking click, but remained stubbornly closed. She sighed, cursing under her breath, and delivered a practiced whack to the side of the machine. With a metallic groan, it conceded defeat, and the drawer popped open.

"Every time!" Mavis chuckled from her seat. "You really need a new one, my dear."

"Already on it, Mavis," Gemma said, counting out the change with a flick of her fingers. "Ordered a fancy new point of sale system. My friend's son, Jack, is setting it up for me soon — the kid's a wizard with all things tech."

"Ah, the joys of modernity," Mavis mused, brushing imaginary lint off her floral blouse.

The day's business had wound down. With an unspoken accord, Gemma and Mavis tidied the shelves and straightened the novels that had been misplaced by capricious customers. Finally, Gemma locked the door of the Bookworm with a satisfied click.

"Ready for a bit of sleuthing later?" Gemma asked with a grin as they walked across the marketplace.

"Oh, always ready, my dear. Let's see Judith at the Mystery Readers' Club first, and then we'll head off," Mavis responded as they approached the entrance to The Swan pub, its windows glowing in the twilight.

Inside, the Mystery Readers' Club was in full swing. Even through the heavy mahogany doors of The Swan's function room, Mavis and Gemma could hear the clink of glasses and the hum of eager conversation.

Judith, the club's president, stood tall and commanding amidst the cheerful chaos. She was wearing a brown cotton dress that came down to her ankles, and her brown hair was tied in a neat knot. She looked keenly at Gemma and Mavis through her half-moon spectacles, as they navigated through the throng of amateur detectives.

"Judith!" Mavis said. "How are you keeping?"

"Mavis! Good to see you. I'm doing very well, thank you."

"We've got an exciting proposition for you."

"I'm all ears."

"How would you feel about moving the Club meetings to the Bookworm?" Mavis said. "We've got more space, and the quiet might be just what this group needs. Cheerful as it is, this function room feels a little cramped, doesn't it?"

"Interesting..." Judith surveyed her surroundings with a critical eye.

Gemma held her breath, waiting for the verdict. Every one of Judith's movements had the quiet gravitas of a judge presiding over the court. It made her look intimidating and slightly comical at the same time.

Mavis leaned in closer to Judith, her voice a conspiratorial whisper. "And imagine, club members could get their hands on our latest mystery arrivals at a discount."

Judith's eyes sparkled. "A larger space, you say?"

"Absolutely," Gemma chimed in. "Our café area is perfect for discussions. And what better ambiance for a Mystery Readers' Club than being surrounded by stacks of crime novels?"

Mavis pulled out the big guns. "Discounted room hire too!"

"Our standard rate is £30 for an evening," said Gemma, "but if you purchase your club books from us at a discount, then we'll rent out the space for £15."

"Very generous," Judith smiled, mulling it over. "But I'd be loath to give up the Swan for just one reason. Our mid-meeting tipple, you know? Our members love a pint with their Poirot."

Gemma beamed. It was time for her *pièce de résistance*. "Oh, funny you should mention that. I've just applied for an alcohol license for the bookshop café. It won't be long before we'll be serving drinks to accompany the debates!"

A slow smile spread across Judith's face. "Really now?" She had long yearned for freedom from the clamour of the pub. "A dedicated space where one can discuss the clues without having to yell? That has a certain appeal."

"Then it's settled?" Gemma extended her hand, her heart thumping with excitement.

"Settled," Judith confirmed, sealing the deal with a firm handshake. "We'll see how the next session goes at the Bookworm!"

"Brilliant!" Gemma couldn't help but break out into a triumphant grin. At least, the future of the Bookworm looked bright and promising — and crowded, the way she had always dreamt of.

"Please stay for this meeting," Judith entreated. "We have quite the debate tonight. And I can sense you both also have a penchant for murder mysteries." Her eyes twinkled mischievously.

"We would love to," Mavis said.

They got a drink from the bar—lime and soda for Gemma as she was driving—and then claimed two worn armchairs at the back of the room. Judith stood at the head of the group, clinking her glass to gain the attention of the chattering members over the noise of the bar.

"Our topic for tonight is," Judith announced with a quiet authority, "The Art of Misdirection. Let's delve into how our author has led us astray with cleverly placed clues and startling plot twists. Who'd like to start?"

A man in a tweed jacket raised his hand, pushing his glasses up the bridge of his nose. "The protagonist's neighbour was mentioned exactly twice before the grand reveal, both times in such an offhand manner that I completely overlooked her significance."

"Ah, but that's the beauty of it, isn't it?" A woman with a cascade of silver curls chimed in. "The signs were there all along, like breadcrumbs. Only, they led in the wrong direction! You have to be a very careful, discerning reader — why, her presence at the garden party in Chapter 5 is *clearly* significant!"

Gemma leaned closer to Mavis. "I would have never caught that on the first read."

"Neither would I," Mavis whispered back, her eyes twinkling with amusement.

"Rubbish!" This impassioned cry came from a rotund gentleman whose face was a shade of salmon pink that matched his tie. "It's not about the neighbour at all! It's the taxidermy owl in the study! On page seventy-eight, it's facing the left. Then on page two hundred twelve, it's suddenly facing the right — clear foreshadowing!"

"Oh, you and your owls, Harold," another member teased. "Next you'll be saying the butler did it because he switched from Earl Grey to Darjeeling!"

The discussion ebbed and flowed around the room, each member presenting their theories with a fervour typically seen only in parliamentary debates. Voices rose at various points, some in defence, others in challenge. And yet the mood remained one of shared passion throughout the meeting, instead of animosity.

"Feisty bunch of readers, aren't they?" Mavis murmured, trying her best to stifle a chuckle.

"Definitely our kind of people," Gemma nodded, already imagining them dissecting plots while munching on Sarah's flapjacks at the Bookworm.

The conversation continued unabated for a full hour. The room echoed with the sounds of passionate, heated discourse. Gemma and Mavis sat back and simply absorbed the lively atmosphere, desperately excited to witness this unfold at the Bookworm. The Club's passion for books, their intricate investigations, and their sleuthing spirit were infectious. They would positively invigorate their quiet, little shop!

As Gemma and Mavis stepped out into the cool evening after the meeting, they could barely contain their admiration.

"Oh, God, Mavis, can you imagine? Our very own mystery club at the Bookworm!" Gemma exclaimed, her voice bubbling with enthusiasm as they crossed the road.

"Quite the coup, my dear," Mavis said. "And just think of the conversations! Poor Harold's owl theories will be loud and clear, not drowned by the pint glasses anymore."

The women shared a laugh as they reached Gemma's car. With a click and a beep, Gemma unlocked the doors, and they settled inside. The engine hummed to life, and Gemma set off toward Sandbed Lane.

A few minutes later, they pulled up in front of Mavis's house. Inside, the quiet hallway was a welcome relief from the bustle and din of the Swan. Mavis and Gemma went straight into the dining room — or, as they called it, their detective headquarters.

"Tea, Gemma?" Mavis asked, already heading toward the kitchen.

"Yes, please," Gemma answered gratefully. "Let's get a good, strong cuppa and crack on with these clues." Five minutes later, Mavis returned bearing a tray with a teapot, two cups, and a plate of chocolate brownies.

"Oh, they look lovely, Mavis. You're spoiling me with your baking," Gemma twinkled.

"Don't worry, my dear, these are healthy ones," Mavis said with a wink. "Banana and chocolate. I made these this morning, before heading to the shop. I mean, we can't solve crimes without some treats, can we? Chocolate fuels the brain!"

Chapter Eighteen

Gemma perched on the edge of a dining chair, her gaze fixed on the white paper taped to the wall. Their makeshift murder board was speckled with the black ink of Mavis' marker pen, her spidery scrawl spread all over. Mavis stood in front of it like an admiral outlining their troop's battle plans.

"Propranolol overdose," she recited, tapping the pen against her chin. "That's what killed Dominic, according to the medical report."

"Yes," Gemma affirmed.

"And Donna's pointing her finger at Ellie."

"That's right. From Donna's perspective, Ellie is the obvious culprit, which we'll come to in a bit. But first, Dominic's house..."

"Let's go through your latest findings in as much detail as we can," said Mavis.

Gemma cast her mind back to the events of the previous day. "The first thing I noticed when I got there with Donna was the reek of bleach in the kitchen. And I mean, it hit you like a punch in the throat," Gemma said. "We had to open the windows to let in some fresh air."

"That amount of bleach, just to clean the house? Sounds excessive," Mavis noted, her pen poised at the ready.

"Exactly. Dominic never went beyond a cursory wipe-down after making coffee, according to Donna. He wasn't a messy person, but this?" Gemma shook her head. "It could be someone trying to erase their presence. Attempting to scrub away fingerprints, or any traces of tampering with the meds."

"I suppose he didn't hire a cleaner?" Mavis asked, jotting down another note on the wall.

"Spot on. Donna said he wouldn't hire a cleaner. But we only have Donna's word for it," said Gemma. "Someone was desperate to clean up evidence. Perhaps evidence of preparing the overdose? It's hard to prove, but I have my suspicions about who might've been scrubbing away their guilt."

"Who?" Mavis asked, clearly intrigued.

"I'll get to that in a bit," Gemma replied. "Let's lay out all the pieces first." Her eyes narrowed as she mentally sifted through their list of suspects.

"Good idea," Mavis said, making a final scribble before capping her pen.

Gemma leaned against the back of a dining chair. "Donna skimmed through Dominic's post while we were there."

"Sounds fair. She has to sort out his financial affairs, after all."

"His post contained bills, final notices, bank statements… all painting a grim portrait of a man drowning in debt."

"Overdrawn?" Mavis's marker hovered by the board.

"Very much so, yeah. Donna seemed shocked to the core," Gemma said. "His book royalties had been substantial at first. Enough that he'd fancied himself a latter-day Hemingway, I suppose, splurging on every whim. But lately, they'd dwindled down to almost nothing. It seems his book isn't the perennial bestseller he thought."

"Quite the reality check for Donna, I imagine," Mavis said, summarising the point with a swift scrawl.

"Exactly. You should've seen her shock, Mavis. The state of his finances completely blindsided her." Gemma's voice softened. "She had no clue about the mountain of debt he'd accumulated."

Mavis added a question mark next to her note before turning back to Gemma. "Poor thing must have been devastated."

"Absolutely gutted," Gemma said, recalling her

shock. She watched Mavis bite on the edge of her pen, lost in thought.

Suddenly, Mavis looked up. "Did she mention any financial troubles of her own?"

"Only in passing. With the cost-of-living crisis biting at her heels, the coaching business isn't thriving, stuff like that." Gemma pulled a brownie towards her and broke off a corner. The scent of dark chocolate mingled with banana filled the air.

"Could it be possible, then," Mavis mused, setting her pen down, "that Donna reconciled with Dominic for financial stability?"

Gemma pondered the question. "I don't think so," she said, taking a bite of the brownie. "You know, I asked her outright why she reconciled with Dominic. Phrased it differently, of course. But her response was... impassioned. There's genuine affection there, I think. Despite everything, she loved him and wanted to make a go of it."

"Love can be a complex motivator," Mavis reflected, picking up her own piece of the banana brownie. "And powerful too."

"True," Gemma said absently. Her eyes suddenly narrowed as she recalled the logs from Dominic's house alarm. "Can I use the pen?"

"Of course."

Gemma wrote the timings of the alarm log entries

on the board, coupled with their fob numbers. She drew a circle around *Fob 3*.

"Mavis, look here," she said, tapping her finger on the wall. Mavis peered over her bifocals.

"What is this, my dear? Something technical?" Mavis asked, mildly apprehensive.

"Quite the opposite. These are entry and exit timings from Dominic's alarm. His alarm is similar to the one we have at the shop, so I knew how to access the logs," Gemma said. "Someone entered the house in the early hours, the morning after Dominic died. Actually, middle of the night is more like it. Here, you see? Dominic used his fob — number one — the last time the house was secured, before going to the bookshop for the reading."

Mavis gave an understanding nod.

"And Donna has number two, which she used the morning we went to the house," Gemma continued, pointing to another entry.

"Then who," Mavis paused for dramatic effect, "has fob three?"

"Exactly. Who has fob three?" Gemma tapped the log again, at an entry the day after Dominic's death. "That could very well be our bleach-loving evidence scrubber."

"Very interesting," Mavis muttered, almost to herself.

"Interesting, right? Now listen to this." Gemma

paced the dining room. "Bill, Dominic's neighbour, saw someone leaving the house the next morning, at about half past five in the morning. The timing matches up with the use of fob three."

Mavis's eyes gleamed. Now *this* was something concrete. "Well, anyone coming and going that early is definitely suspicious."

"Which leads to my hunch. Bill said it was a young man, but his face was concealed by a large hoodie. Also said the man didn't seem furtive at all. He seemed confident, in fact. Which is why Bill wasn't overly suspicious at the time, even though it was so early," Gemma said. "Do you remember seeing a young man at the funeral, lurking in the back? He was also dressed in a hoodie, right?"

"Yes, I remember the lad, The logic seems sound, you know. Could this be our murderer?" Mavis asked gravely.

"It is definitely a possibility," Gemma admitted. "Bill didn't think anything of it because the man locked up properly and walked away. According to him, it seemed 'normal', as if he had every right to be there."

"Curiouser and curiouser," Mavis murmured, echoing the words of one of her favourite childhood reads. But unlike Alice's adventures in Wonderland, they were going down a rabbit hole of much darker truths.

"So now, the key is to find out who this boy is," Mavis stated. "But how do we go about it?" Her gaze lingered on the murder board for a minute. Then she sighed and shuffled off towards the kitchen.

"More tea?" she called over her shoulder. Gemma just nodded, even though Mavis couldn't see her.

The click of the kettle signalled Mavis's return to the dining table. She set down a fresh teapot and two cups beside the half-eaten brownies. She slowly poured steaming tea into the cups, and added a splash of milk.

Gemma blew at the cup, took a sip, and then set it down.

"I didn't tell you about Geoff Dunsworth's visit," she said after a brief pause.

"Geoff Dunsworth? He's the local builder, isn't he?"

"The same. He showed up unannounced and bulldozed his way into the kitchen, when Donna and I were discussing finances."

"Must've given you quite the fright."

"It did. Unnerving is an understatement. Turns out Dominic owed him a hefty sum — £30,000, for the new kitchen and extension. Geoff was seething. Said he needed the money to pay his labourers, and now he's demanding Donna settle the debt. He's given her one week."

"Quite the pickle," Mavis mused, reaching for another brownie.

"Exactly."

"Especially with the state of Dominic's finances... Whatever will the poor woman do?"

Mavis capped her marker with a decisive click and turned to Gemma, who was still seated at the dining table covered in brownie crumbs.

"Gemma... Do you think Geoff could commit murder over the outstanding money?" she asked.

Gemma shrugged. "I'm not sure, to be honest. What's the point of murdering the person who owes you money?" The thought seemed counterintuitive. After all, the dead can't settle debts.

"That's true enough," Mavis conceded, "but consider this, my dear. Upon that person's death, the will would be executed, and he could make a claim to have the debt paid off from the estate."

"That's actually an excellent motive for murder, if he couldn't get Dominic to pay up," Gemma realised. It was an angle they hadn't explored yet — and it painted Geoff Dunsworth in a more sinister light.

"But then, if he was the murderer, he wouldn't barge in at the house like that, would he?"

"Would be a good deflection. But, yes, it would be really reckless."

"I don't think he was in the house the day after the death, though," Gemma said. "Unless he had that missing alarm fob — but he certainly couldn't be mistaken for a young man, or a teenager."

"He could've sent one of his labourers to the house to do a tidy up on his behalf. Or even taken things into his own hands, since the debt hadn't been paid," Mavis proposed.

Gemma smiled. "You know what? That's feasible, Mavis. We should try to find out who he works with. What we can't rule out is that Geoff wasn't at the house the day before — when Dominic was there, I mean. Unfortunately, Dominic didn't have any security cameras."

"I'll add this to the board," said Mavis, standing up. She took the pen and scribbled notes under Geoff's name. Gemma suddenly exclaimed.

"Oh, I nearly forgot! Donna told me Ellie worked in that large coffee shop on King Street," she recalled, drumming her finger on the table.

"Ah, yes. She's still a bit of an enigma, isn't she?"

"Donna is still convinced that Ellie has something to do with Dominic's death. I'm not so sure," Gemma sighed.

"That's only natural, isn't it? Donna's grasping at straws, looking for someone to blame. A natural part of the grieving process."

"That's true enough. She could also just be jealous of Ellie — especially if it was Ellie that Dominic cheated with behind her back," Gemma said. "You know, Mavis, I think we should try to talk to Ellie in person. Hear her side of the story. After all, we can't base everything on Donna's testimony alone."

"I agree," Mavis said, already planning her approach.

"I'm not working at the Bookworm tomorrow. I'll pop into the coffee shop, see if I can chat with Ellie. Or at least introduce myself. Try to find something about her."

"Subtle as always, Mavis," Gemma chuckled. Her straightforward questions might just be what they needed to get some answers.

Mavis peered over her glasses, a frown creasing her forehead. "Gemma, if we were to get down to brass tacks... could Donna have done it?" she asked, tapping the marker against her chin.

Gemma hesitated, scratching her head. "Donna's in dire straits, Mavis. Not that we've seen the will, but it's likely the house would have gone to her. We have no idea if Dominic removed her from his will after she left. I would, if it was me," she admitted, biting her lip.

"Money does strange things to people," Mavis replied.

"True, but Donna was away just before the murder," Gemma pointed out. "She spent a few nights in York for a friend's birthday, and didn't return until the next morning." She tried to recall what Donna had said about her trip. "She even stopped at a service station on her way back."

"Hard for us to confirm," Mavis said, scribbling a note. "The police will need to look into that, I suppose."

"Exactly," Gemma agreed, feeling a knot form in her

stomach. Accusing someone of murder was no small matter.

Mavis and Gemma stepped back to survey their evening's work. The dining room wall, once bare, now looked like a detective's case-board, plastered with notes and timelines. Copious question marks hovered over suspect names.

"That's it, then. I'll see what I can find out from the coffee shop tomorrow morning," Mavis declared.

"Good plan," Gemma replied, her own resolve solidifying. "We need all the information we can get." She made her way to the front door, feeling pleased, and maybe a little excited. They had finally made some headway — done something concrete.

"Good night, Mavis. This was fun."

"'Night, Gemma. I'll report in once I have been for coffee at that shop," Mavis said. "Buying coffee from a competitor, whatever shall we have to do next?"

Gemma chuckled. "See you, Mavis!"

She stepped out into the warm night air.

Chapter Nineteen

Mavis pushed open the glass door of The Roasted Bean, the bustling coffee shop on King Street. The moment she set foot inside the spotless interior, the rich, nutty fragrance of coffee enveloped her. It was an energising, bittersweet aroma, that instantly woke up your senses.

The Roasted Bean was a sprawling space, almost twice as big as the Bookworm, but just as cosy. The small tables were surrounded by comfy chairs and sofas, and lush green plants dotted every corner. Patrons stood in a queue, ordering their morning brew from a large chalk-board menu behind the counter, and there were stacks of fresh pastries on display.

Weaving through the chattering patrons, Mavis's eyes went behind the counter where young baristas produced cups of coffee with the expertise of alchemists.

These weren't just the regular espressos or cappuccinos. To her bewilderment, the baristas whipped up colourful concoctions with generous syrups, sprinkles, and even ice in one — whatever happened to good old-fashioned *coffee*?

Focusing on the task at hand, she quickly scanned the name badges pinned to the brown aprons until they landed on Ellie — a tall, lithe young lady with a blonde ponytail that swayed as she worked the espresso machine. Mavis took her place in the queue.

"Next, please," Ellie sang out cheerfully. Mavis stepped forward, mustering her most congenial smile.

"Good morning! I'll have a latte, and one of those scrumptious-looking cinnamon buns, please."

"Coming right up."

As Ellie prepared the order, Mavis introduced herself. "I'm sure you don't know me, my dear, but I work at the bookshop down the street. The Bookworm, it's called. I was acquainted with Dominic Westley," she launched straight into the offensive.

Ellie's hands halted for a few seconds, and then she hurriedly resumed her task. "I see," she murmured, avoiding Mavis's gaze.

"I noticed you at the funeral," Mavis continued, adept at treading delicate ground. "You were quite hidden in the back. I wondered... is everything okay, my dear?"

Ellie slid the steaming latte across the counter, along

with the cinnamon bun on a plate. She glanced around the shop, then leaned in closer. "You— you knew Dominic?" she whispered.

"I did, yes. I lived near him, on Sandbed Lane. We invited him to the shop, for a reading of his book."

"Could we... talk?" Ellie entreated. "I have a break in ten minutes."

"Of course, my dear." Mavis smiled. Mission accomplished.

With the warm cup cradled in her hands, Mavis wandered over to a quiet corner of the shop. She settled into an overstuffed armchair, broke off a piece of the cinnamon bun, and waited for Ellie to join her.

Mavis had always had a knack for encouraging confidences. It was her motherly, slightly vague demeanour that compelled people to confide in her — and she took some pains to cultivate that air of flustered concern, for this very purpose. You could know a lot about a person if you simply offered a sympathetic ear.

After a little while, Ellie finally approached the quiet corner, her smile cautious but genuine. "Thank you for waiting, we had a sudden surge in customers," she said apologetically, settling into the chair opposite Mavis.

"That's no problem, my dear," said Mavis. "Customer service is unpredictable, as I know only too well."

Ellie gave a warm grin. "Ellie Simpson," she said, offering her hand. "Dominic is my boyfriend. Well, *was...*"

Mavis's eyes softened, and she patted the proffered hand kindly. "My condolences for your loss, Ellie. It must be very difficult."

Ellie's eyes glistened. "Thank you."

"Forgive me for being so forward," Mavis began, her tone the usual blend of curiosity and concern, "but if you were Dominic's partner, why were you tucked away so furtively at the funeral? Surely, you had every right to be there."

Ellie exhaled, averting her eyes. "I wasn't exactly... invited," she admitted. "Donna, his ex-wife, well... she thinks I'm the reason their marriage fell apart."

"Ah," Mavis sighed, the sound soft but loaded with understanding. She leaned forward. "And what did you think, my dear?"

Ellie nervously laced and unlaced her fingers, as though gathering her resolve. "I just wanted to be with him," she said at length.

"My dear, were you with Dominic before he parted ways with Donna?" Mavis asked softly.

Ellie fidgeted with the hem of her apron. "Oh no, not at all. It really wasn't like that! Dominic was already separated from Donna when we started seeing each other." Her voice was barely audible.

"Do you know the lady he was involved with before you?"

"To be honest, no. Dominic always referred to it as a careless fling. A mistake. He never even mentioned her name, just brushed it off like it was nothing important. Towards the end, I'm almost certain he just kind of... forgot about it." Her gaze shifted, fixing on a spot on the table.

"We lived together, you know. And ludicrous as it might sound, I was happy," Ellie continued, with the air of someone finally letting go of a heavy burden. "I was in love, really in love. I believed we were building something— *real*!" Her voice faltered.

"Did something happen to change that?" Mavis asked.

Ellie's lip trembled. "I told him I was pregnant."

The words hung in the air. It was as if someone hit the mute button on the noise and bustle of the crowded café for a few moments. Only Ellie's words echoed, reverberating through the cosy corner where they sat. Tears brimmed in Mavis's eyes. She reached out and placed a comforting hand over Ellie's.

"Children are a blessing, my dear."

Her voice was soft and comforting, but there was an edge in it. She seemed to be willing her words to be true, not just for herself, but for the young woman before her, caught amidst the crosswinds of love and loss.

Her attempt to conceal her shock under a veil of composure was only partially successful. Mavis swallowed the lump in her throat, and applied herself anew to the conversation.

"And what was Dominic's reaction? I'm sure he

must have been over the moon," she prodded. But despite her words, Mavis was a woman of the world. She knew better.

Ellie made a rueful grimace. "Happy? Far from it," she hissed. "He lost his temper, accused me of being reckless. He blamed me. As if I were the only one responsible!" She shook her head, her eyes darkening at the memory.

"Dominic even— he pushed for a termination," Ellie confessed in a tremulous whisper, "but that's something I couldn't do. It's against everything I believe in."

She paused and wiped a few tears from her eyes. "He even promised me that if I had a termination now, we could get engaged later and... and have a baby when the time was right."

"Goodness," Mavis murmured. "And when you stood by your beliefs, how did he take it?"

Ellie laughed. It was a hollow, bitter laugh, devoid of any humour. "Like a storm brewing over the dales," she replied. "He erupted. Told me to pack my bags and leave — 'our home' wasn't mine anymore."

Her hands trembled, and she clasped them tightly in her lap. "I was scared, Mavis. Truly scared. So I did what he asked. I packed what little I could and went to a friend's place. What else could I do?"

Mavis was speechless. Her heart ached at the thought of the young woman before her, utterly alone and vulnerable.

"You left without a proper plan?" she asked.

Memories from those first few years after poor Fred departed came rushing back. What would she herself have done without the kind support of her family, her loved ones? She felt a pang of sorrow for Ellie.

"Didn't have the luxury of a plan," Ellie gave another rueful smile. "After a few days, once the dust had settled, I called Dominic about the rest of my things. He told me I could come and pick them up." A shadow passed across her face. "But there was no reconciliation, no softening on his part — just cold civility. Not even a sense of responsibility, nor any concern for me."

Ellie's gaze drifted past Mavis. "I had this foolish hope," she went on, her voice a mere whisper, "that Dominic might have cooled off, maybe even felt a twinge of regret." She scoffed. "But when I got there, the first thing he said to me was whether I'd changed my mind about the termination."

Mavis's jaw dropped in indignation. How could a person be so callous, so unfeeling?

"I hadn't, of course," Ellie continued, her eyes reflecting a firm resolve. "So, I didn't say a word, and just gathered the rest of my things. Everything I owned — my clothes, my books, photographs of my family, the earrings my mum gave me on my 18th — every single little bit of my life was with him, in his house. And he just stood in a corner, watching as if I were a stranger!" Her voice rose, and then abruptly broke.

"Did he say anything then?"

"Only when I was leaving." A bitter laugh escaped Ellie's mouth. "He demanded his keys back. And he got them, alright, hurled right at his feet. I stormed out, didn't look back."

Mavis nodded thoughtfully. She could feel the sorrow, the pain, the indignation rippling in waves from Ellie's very person. There was no need to ask how she'd felt. Instead, Mavis simply asked, "And after that?"

"Haven't spoken to him since," Ellie admitted, tucking a stray lock of hair behind her ear. "A mutual friend told me that Dominic was back with Donna, not long after our split. He'd started patching things up with her. It felt like a stab to the heart. Here I was, my life turned upside down, and he was going back to his old one, as if— as if I was just a detour."

"Seems like he had a knack for landing on his feet," Mavis remarked. "Before his untimely demise, of course," she added hurriedly. She knew, only too well, how shockingly unfair love and life could be.

"Exactly," Ellie said. "That's exactly it. He was always Dominic the renowned author — always unscathed and upright, no matter who he hurt, or the mess he left behind."

Sitting in that quiet corner of the bustling coffeeshop, Mavis pondered on the irony of it all. Here was Ellie, dignified, upright, and loving, yet discarded and utterly alone. While Dominic — callous, arrogant and thoughtless — had seemed to escape every consequence throughout his life. He loved, hurt and discarded women as he saw fit, yet both of those women still mourned him, and bore the consequences of his actions. It was almost comical in its pathos.

Mavis reached across the table, her fingers instinctively brushing away a crumb from her cinnamon bun. "And how is the baby, my dear?" she asked, her voice laced with genuine concern.

"Five months along now," Ellie smiled, resting a protective hand on her stomach. "The scans show a healthy little one."

"That's wonderful to hear!" Mavis said warmly. She paused, collecting her thoughts before venturing further. "How did you feel when you heard about Dominic?"

Ellie sighed, closing her eyes. "Upset, of course. My baby will grow up without a daddy. Although, at least..." she paused. "At least now they won't know that daddy didn't want them!" she said, suddenly bursting into tears. Mavis patted her arm comfortingly. After a few moments, Ellie looked up, wiped her tears, and pulled herself together.

"I'm sorry. It's complicated. I hated him for what he did to me, but..." she trailed off, lost in a whirlwind of conflicting emotions.

Mavis gave a gentle nod. "And the funeral?" she prompted, sensing there was something more than grief troubling Ellie.

"I wasn't invited," Ellie said, bitterness seeping into her tone. "I'm sure that Donna believes I'm the woman he cheated on her with. But I swear, it's not true, Mavis! I wasn't. I wouldn't ever do that, you know... wreck a home. When Dominic and I got together, he was single. Free as a bird, or so he claimed. We were a serious couple, and we lived together." She shrugged, in a futile attempt to dismiss the pain.

Mavis lightly touched Ellie's arm. "I'm truly sorry you've had to endure all this, Ellie. I can only imagine how hard it is on you."

"Thank you," Ellie murmured, meeting the older woman's eyes gratefully. "Really, you don't know how much it means to unburden myself like this, Mavis."

"If ever you need someone to talk to, or just fancy a change of scenery, the Bookworm is always open to you," Mavis said, thinking of the quiet nooks between shelves that were perfect for heart-to-heart conversations.

Ellie's face brightened for a moment. "I might just take you up on that. Thank you."

She glanced reluctantly at the clock on the wall. "Time for me to get back to work, I'm afraid." She stood up, smoothing the apron over her incipient baby bump. "Thanks for the chat, Mavis."

"It was a pleasure. Sorry to have taken up all your coffee break, though," Mavis replied, pushing her chair back and rising to her feet.

"I don't mind at all," Ellie smiled. "While you're here, would you like another coffee?"

"I'd best not. Keeps me up at night. Thank you, though, my dear."

Ellie nodded and headed back to the counter.

As Mavis left the coffee shop, her mind was a hive of activity, buzzing with information and conjectures. All that she'd learned this afternoon would help them fill in quite a lot of blanks!

She couldn't wait to tell Gemma everything.

Chapter Twenty

Gemma was perched on a stool behind the counter of the Bookworm. It was Mavis's day off, which meant she had to tend to the quiet hum of the shop alone.

The bell above the door was keeping up a steady chime today as a trickle of customers meandered in, each one drawn to the same section. They left clutching copies of *Paper Boats in the Monsoon* by the late Dominic Westley. Apparently, his recent tragic demise had propelled his work to new heights of popularity. The author himself would have revelled in this posthumous surge of sales, Gemma was certain.

She was startled out of these ruminations by a loud noise. The entry bell clanged with more force than usual as a delivery driver, framed by the doorway, heaved in a large box with a grunt and a good-natured smile.

"Delivery for the Bookworm," the driver announced, setting the parcel down with a thud, and wiping his forehead with the back of his hand. Gemma knew what it was.

"Thank you!" she said, hopping from her stool to greet him. "It's the new point-of-sale system!" She eagerly scribbled her signature across the digital pad with a stylus that had evidently seen better days. "This cash register's been on its last legs for far too long."

"Looks like technology is catching up with you here!" the delivery man chuckled, eyeing the antiquated cash register that sat on the counter like a relic.

"It is, indeed," Gemma declared. The driver doffed his cap and disappeared back into the street. Alone again, she grasped the edges of the box and shuffled it behind the counter with a slightly awkward push and pull.

Then, Gemma took out her phone, and thumbed through her contacts, the glow of the device casting a soft light on her face.

"It's here, Jack! When can you set up the new cash register?" She typed out the message and hit send.

"Sunday work?" Jack's immediate response blinked into view. *"Takes time to install."*

"*Perfect.*" Gemma typed back, her lips curving into an eager smile. "*We only open for a few hours on Sunday, so I'll just close shop. See you then!*"

With her Sunday plans made, Gemma tucked her

phone away. She glanced around the nearly empty bookshop and made her way to the café, where Sarah was wiping down the counters.

"Everything alright, Sarah?" Gemma asked, observing the young woman's movements. She seemed just a tad restless and her usual cheerfulness was dimmed down. Sarah looked up, her face framed by strands of hair that had escaped her low ponytail.

"Could be better, I suppose," she said, leaning against the counter. "To tell you the truth, I haven't been sleeping well the past couple of days. Feeling a little under the weather."

"I'm sorry to hear that." Gemma gave a sympathetic cluck. "You think it's a bug?"

"Could be," Sarah replied, stifling a yawn. "I just hope it's nothing serious."

"You can take your Sunday morning shift off," Gemma suggested, leaning against the counter. "We're going to install the new point-of-sale system, so the shop will be closed. And looks like you could definitely use a good rest."

A weary smile spread across Sarah's features. "Really? Oh, that'd be lovely, Gemma. Thanks!"

"Of course," Gemma smiled, pushing herself off the counter. "The café is our main line of defence, and you're the general. We need you in top form! So rest up and get better."

"Will do."

Taking up her post behind the counter once again, Gemma found herself pleasantly surprised. A sudden, late-afternoon rush had filled the bookshop with a gentle hum of activity. A stream of customers fluttered amidst the shelves, their fingers dancing along the spines of well-loved classics and newly printed mysteries alike.

Gemma prepared to wage battle with the cash register again. Thankfully, only a few more days and she'd be spared its tantrums forevermore. Customers soon queued up by the counter, eagerly clutching their chosen books.

"Another copy of Mr Westley's book? That's the sixth one today," Gemma remarked to a regular patron. This renewed surge in Dominic's sales wasn't going to die down soon. Gemma pondered whether the increased royalties would be of some help to poor Donna.

"Can't wait to read it," the woman replied, clutching the book to her chest. "It's as if he's speaking to us from beyond, isn't it?"

"Quite the legacy to leave behind," Gemma said, absently thumping the cash drawer to give the customer her change.

By late afternoon, the shop had returned to its usual tranquillity. Soon, the last customer waved goodbye, their new read tucked under an arm. Gemma watched as Sarah methodically wiped down tables with a rag of cloth, and lined up chairs with the precision of a drill sergeant. The café was positively spotless under her care, ready for whatever the next day might bring.

"Looks great, Sarah," she called out, admiring the pristine cleanliness. Whatever would she do without Sarah!

"Thanks," she replied with a hint of pride. "I'm off then."

"See you tomorrow!"

Alone now, Gemma went to the door with a contented sigh and, with a flick of her wrist, flipped the sign to 'Closed'. The lock clicked, securing her world of books behind her.

She strolled across the marketplace to the Coppice carpark, where her car awaited. The keys jingled in her hand as she walked.

Gemma slipped inside her VW Beetle, started the engine, and drove off. She could already picture Mavis's animated stories and delicious bakes, punctuated by the joyful barks of an eager Baxter.

Chapter Twenty-One

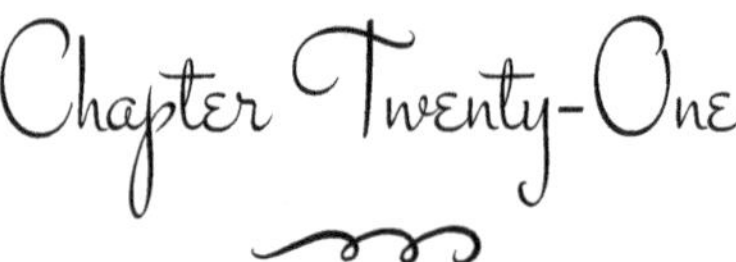

Gemma eased her car to a gentle stop in front of Mavis's house. Baxter, the embodiment of canine patience, sat upright on the backseat, his tail thumping in anticipation. He had come to know this ritual well — it was time for walkies.

A sound of locks clicking into place heralded the arrival of Mavis, who emerged from her front door eagerly dangling a bag of chocolate cookies from her fingertips.

"Come on, Baxter!" Gemma called, pushing open the car door. The dog needed no further invitation. He bounded out eagerly and Gemma clipped on his lead.

"Couldn't have asked for a better day!" Mavis declared, holding up the bag with a flourish. "And wait till you try these — a new recipe."

They ambled down the path together, the two

women strolling slowly while Baxter scampered ahead and sniffed everything in sight. As they turned right onto Bargate Road, the full panorama of Belper presented itself. Lush green hills stretched out as far as the eye could see. Verdant fields and thick woods surrounded Belper, nestled as it was in the Amber Valley. Gemma and Mavis paused for a moment to take in the true glory of their sleepy little town. Then, prodded by Baxter, they walked down the road towards a park.

A group of local kids was engaged in a spirited football match. The thuds of the ball and calls of "Pass it!" filled the air. Mavis smiled as she passed the cookies to Gemma.

"Try one of these, my dear."

"Twist my arm, why don't you?" Gemma replied with mock reluctance, taking a bite.

The cookie was divine. Crisp on the outside, and still gooey in the middle. By now, their stroll had taken them to the secluded end of the park, where a gap in the bushes beckoned them onto a less-trodden path — a farmer's track that meandered through the surrounding spring barley fields, where time seemed to unfold at its own leisurely pace. Here, Baxter's leash was removed, and he skipped ahead with unbridled joy.

"Look at him go," Gemma said with a chuckle, watching Baxter zigzag frantically across the open land, nose inches above the ground, ears flopping.

"He's got the right idea!" Mavis said, her eyes

following Baxter as he undoubtedly searched for rabbits.

As they ambled down the farmer's track, Mavis grew pensive, her eyes narrowing in a way that Gemma recognised as the precursor to significant news. She prepared herself for the upcoming information, and kept an eye on Baxter who, oblivious to human affairs, was chasing around an unsuspecting butterfly.

"I spoke to Ellie this morning at the coffee shop," Mavis began, her voice casual but with an undercurrent of excitement. "Got some really interesting information about Dominic."

Gemma's ears perked up. "Oh? Do tell!"

"First off, Donna's completely mistaken. Ellie is positive that Dominic was single when she met him. So Donna's allegation of her being a home wrecker is all poppycock."

"Interesting," Gemma mused. "So that means Donna's theory flies right out of the window, right?"

"Wait until you hear the rest," Mavis interjected, her tone dropping to a whisper so Gemma had to lean in closer to listen. "Their relationship... It hit a rather rocky patch."

"Can't say I'm surprised," Gemma shrugged. "Do you know why they split?"

"Can you guess why?" Mavis asked. The quiet indignation in her eyes sparked Gemma's curiosity. She thought for a minute and then shook her head.

"Ellie's pregnant."

Gemma stopped in her tracks, her mouth agape.

"Pregnant? But..."

"Exactly." Mavis nodded. "And when she told Dominic, he was livid. Even had the nerve to suggest—" she broke off, glancing around before leaning in again, "—a termination!"

"Gosh, Mavis, that's appalling!" Gemma gasped. "Dominic was no gentleman. Poor Ellie."

They walked on, their steps slower as both of them grappled with the gravity of poor Ellie's situation. Baxter, with his nose to the ground, led them farther along the farmer's track, pulled forward by a curious scent. Gemma watched her pet with a smile, but her thoughts were directed back to the troubling conversation.

"When she refused to terminate the pregnancy, Dominic broke up with her. And pretty much turned her out of his house, too. But she returned a few days later to collect her possessions," Mavis said. "She was hoping Dominic had a change of heart about the baby."

"And had he?" Gemma asked, although she suspected she already knew the answer.

"Far from it," Mavis huffed. "He demanded to know if she'd reconsidered... you know, getting rid of the baby." She shook her head, disgust registered plainly on her face.

Gemma felt her heart ache for Ellie. "So, he essentially refused to take any responsibility at all? Oh Mavis, that's shocking indeed!"

The acclaimed literary genius Dominic Westley — Gemma had thought that arrogance and pompousness were the worst flaws he had. But such heartlessness? She regretted ever having sold any of his books. She wondered what would happen if the public knew about his indiscretions. Would they still queue up to buy his book and hear him *speak from beyond the grave*?

Mavis saw her friend's pensive face. She reached into her bag and handed a chocolate cookie to her.

"Domestic bliss turned sour," Gemma said. The taste of the chocolate almost managed to calm her thoughts, but not quite. "She could have killed him out of rage, for abandoning her and the baby. It *is* a motive, but it doesn't feel like a strong one, does it?"

"No, it doesn't, my dear. It feels a bit too dramatic," Mavis agreed. "Even if she did feel vengeful, what would killing Dominic accomplish from her point of view? And Ellie told me Dominic made her give the keys back. So she wouldn't have had access to the house, after all."

"That makes sense." Gemma paused. "Besides, knowing you're bringing a life into this world, would you risk it all by taking one? Seems odd, doesn't it?"

"Very odd," Mavis concurred. "And let me tell you, Ellie is an eminently sensible girl — even in distress."

They walked on, digesting this new piece of the puzzle.

Gravel and dead leaves crunched underfoot. The mystery seemed to be unfurling in unforeseen ways, just like the path before them. Gemma watched as Baxter bounded ahead, a blur of furry enthusiasm among the underbrush. Her thoughts, however, remained tethered to the conversation.

She broke the silence after a few minutes. "She might not have had the opportunity, but she had the means. Ellie knew enough about Dominic's health to do him harm if she wished to."

Mavis nodded. "That's true enough. Living together lays bare many secrets — including what's in one's medicine cabinet."

"True, she'd know how to..." Gemma trailed off, the word '*murder*' sticking in her throat. "What about opportunity, though? If Ellie didn't have the keys, it isn't likely that she could have snuck in and tampered with Dominic's medication."

"Quite so. I don't think that theory holds water."

"Unless Ellie was lying about returning the keys."

"Perhaps," Mavis conceded, though her tone was doubtful. "But my instinct says she was sincere. She was clearly devastated by the entire ordeal."

"Devastated enough to fabricate a story?" Gemma pointed out. She harboured reservations about such deceit from Ellie as well, but she was determined not to make the mistake of being too trusting.

"Hard to say," Mavis answered. "But Ellie's heartbreak seemed genuine, and I've seen enough sorrow in my time to recognise its true face."

Gemma nodded absentmindedly. Mavis had much greater experience in these matters, and she was content to trust in her authority. Silence settled over them again, broken only by the crunch of their footsteps on the gravel, and Baxter's contented panting.

At last, Gemma spoke up. "But that still doesn't clear up the matter of the boy seen leaving Dominic's house. It clearly couldn't have been Ellie. I mean, even if she's lying about the keys, as pregnant as she is..." she cut herself off, watching Baxter chase his tail with abandon.

"Quite right," Mavis chimed in, adjusting her spectacles with a thoughtful tap. "It'd be impossible to mistake a five-month pregnant woman for a teenage boy in a hoodie, even with bad eyesight."

Baxter trotted over, his tongue lolling out in a pant that seemed almost like a laugh. Once he was by their side, they turned around, retracing their steps towards the park.

"That reminds me," Mavis started as they navigated the narrow farmer's track, "I had quite the conversation at the post office today."

"Anything that might help us with our little puzzle?"

"Potentially. It was about the builder, Geoff Dunsworth."

"What about him?"

Mavis's next words landed with the weight of a sledgehammer. "He's not just your average tradesman. Did a stint in prison. For GBH, no less."

"Good heavens!" Gemma gasped. "That certainly paints our Mr. Dunsworth in a different light!"

"It does indeed," Mavis nodded. "I think we should add him as a definite suspect. Owed a hefty sum, and he has a dangerous temper, it seems. He had access to the house too, while working on the extension and kitchen."

"Opportunity and motive then, albeit a bit thin. But what about means?" Gemma asked, staring in the distance as she pictured Geoff's rough, callused hands. They were powerful enough to build homes. Were they capable of something darker too? "Did he know enough about Dominic's condition to meddle?"

"An excellent question, my dear," Mavis stated. "And one we can't answer just yet."

Their stroll continued, its pace quickening as the sun set. The fading daylight cast long shadows over the fields.

Their conversation dwindled as they approached Mavis's house. The walk had been illuminating, if not chilling — each revelation had added layers of poignancy to an already tragic, convoluted mystery. Gemma clicked open the car door, and Baxter, ever the obedient companion, hopped into the backseat.

"By the way," Gemma said as she secured Baxter's

lead to the safety hook, "The new point-of-sale system arrived today. Jack's coming around on Sunday to set it all up. Fancy popping in? We'll be closed to the public, but I could use some company."

Mavis, who had been watching Baxter settle in with an affectionate smile, turned her keen eyes to Gemma. "Oh certainly, I'd love that. We can have a good natter, without customers interrupting us every five minutes."

"Brilliant!" Gemma said.

She slid into the driver's seat, ready to head home. Suddenly, she leaned out of the window. "Are you going to update the murder board?"

"Of course," Mavis chuckled, her thoughts already dancing around the clues and conjectures they'd amassed. "I'll update it with today's— discoveries."

"Good night, Mavis!" Gemma called out, waving back before starting her car.

As Gemma pulled away, she glanced in the rear-view to see Mavis heading towards her front door.

Chapter Twenty-Two

The morning sun had only just begun its slow ascent over the horizon, and the languid rooftops of Belper were bathed in a gentle, golden glow. The marketplace, usually a flurry of activity, resembled a placid lake as Gemma approached her bookshop.

It was Sunday, a day when the Bookworm welcomed readers who wanted to spend a tranquil morning in the quiet embrace of stories. But today, the doors were to remain closed. It was time for the Bookworm to get an update — to catch up with the pace of the outside world.

Gemma fished out her keys and unlocked the door with a satisfying click.

"I would love a nice cup of coffee," Mavis quipped, approaching the doorstep.

"Definitely."

Gemma ushered her companion into the cosy embrace of the shop. As she flipped on the lights, the shelves seemed to awaken from their slumber. She set about making coffee, the machine sputtering as it worked its magic. Mavis perched herself atop one of the high stools by the counter.

They were waiting for Jack, a bright-eyed youth in his early twenties, who had agreed to bring the establishment into the modern age with the new point-of-sale system. He was the son of Gemma's best friend, and her knight in shining armour for all things technology.

The smell of freshly brewed coffee soon filled the air, and the bell above the door signalled Jack's arrival. He was tall and slim with brown hair that was cropped short, and wore ripped blue jeans, and a black heavy metal t-shirt.

"Morning, Jack! Thanks for helping today, I really appreciate it," Gemma said with genuine gratitude. "Mavis, this is Jack. He's our very own tech wizard."

"Lovely to meet you," Mavis said, offering a hand to Jack.

He seemed a bit taken aback, as if he wasn't quite used to the formality, but he took her hand and shook it politely.

"Would you like a coffee?" Mavis asked.

"Yes, please. Black with three sugars," Jack replied.

"Jack here works over at the sorting office on Goods Road," Gemma explained.

"I'm happy to help," Jack assured them, smiling. "I love tinkering with tech. It's like solving a puzzle — and I get to save the day without wearing a cape!"

Gemma chuckled at this analogy. "Well, we're truly grateful. Just being able to open the cash drawer without resorting to violence will make my days!" She led Jack to the counter, and pointed to an unopened box on the floor. "The future of our bookkeeping is in there!"

Jack wasted no time. With a few swift movements, he cleared the old cash register off the counter, and dove into the box with the eagerness of a child opening presents on Christmas morning.

While Jack busied himself with cables and components, Gemma retreated to the café. The coffee machine whirred as she prepared the drinks and she selected the plumpest Belgium bun from the pastry cabinet, its sugary glaze twinkling under the white light.

"Here we go, something to fuel your grey cells," she said, placing the food beside Jack, as he admired the sleek touchscreen of the point-of-sale system.

"Cheers, Gemma," he said, reaching out for the bun, his eyes still glued to the screen.

The next moment, the screen flickered to life, casting a soft glow on Jack's face. He turned to Gemma, his eyes alight with excitement.

"So, this little gadget," he said, lifting a hand

terminal that looked as if it belonged on a star ship rather than in a quaint bookshop, "is going to change your world."

"Really?" Gemma leaned in closer, slightly bewildered.

"Yes! You can scan every book in the store, input the number of copies you have, and voila! The system keeps track of your stock, and even helps with reordering when stocks run low!"

Gemma nodded in awe. She pictured a world where inventory didn't mean sifting through piles of books and scribbling down numbers for hours.

"Oh, that's brilliant!" she exclaimed. "You don't know how difficult it is to manage stock!" She'd never been adept at managing her stock. Books always seemed to vanish, or multiplied at will. But with this new system and Jack's explanation, her shop would run like clockwork — each title accounted for, each author properly shelved. It was almost too good to be true.

Seated on a pair of stools, Mavis and Gemma leaned forward to watch Jack's nimble fingers fly over the keyboard. The new point-of-sale system, its screen aglow with crisp graphics, hummed to life under his touch. With a few final taps, Jack straightened up and grinned at them.

"Right, it's all set up," he said. "Now it just needs to download the latest updates." He ran a hand through his untidy hair. "That shouldn't take too long."

"Thank you, Jack, really," Gemma said with a grateful smile. "This is going to make such a huge difference!"

The computer began its silent work, downloading bytes of data, while Jack tapped away at the keyboard. Mavis turned her attention to Gemma, signalling her to come to the café.

"Speaking of mysteries," Mavis ventured, "have you thought more about whether our suspects could have done such a dreadful deed?"

Gemma bit her lip, her gaze drifting towards the rows of colourful books on the nearby 'Biographies' shelf. "Honestly, Mavis, I don't think any of them could do it. It's just my instinct, but none of our suspects seems likely."

"Ellie's expecting. Wilful murder wouldn't exactly be the wisest move for her," Mavis said in a pensive tone.

"Exactly," Gemma replied, nodding. "Why would she do anything like that when she has a child on the way? That would ruin both their lives. She'd be in prison, and then what would happen to the baby? Not to mention, what would be the point of killing Dominic, provided she didn't stand to gain anything by his will?"

"And Donna?" Mavis pressed on, her tone suggesting she was far from convinced of anyone's innocence.

"Despite everything, she seemed to really love

Dominic," Gemma said. "She has financial worries, sure, but after spending time with her... I don't know, Mavis, I can't sense any hate."

Mavis's gaze settled on a photograph of Dominic, on the jacket of his book. His smile was now frozen in time. "Human hearts are complicated things," she said, looking up from the book.

Gemma nodded. Yet as they sat there, the gentle whirr of the computer blending with the ticking of the old clock on the wall, the two women shared a moment of silent understanding. The truth, much like the perfect ending to a mystery novel, was simply waiting to be uncovered.

Gemma watched as Mavis's eyebrow arched, a signal that the gears in her mind were turning at full speed. "So, we've ticked off the women. That just leaves our mystery boy and the disgruntled builder, doesn't it?"

"Geoff Dunsworth," Gemma said. She couldn't shake the image of the burly builder threatening Donna. "With his history of violence..." she paused, realising the gravity of the situation for the first time. "And Dominic owed him a really hefty sum. Could be motive enough for someone already on the edge."

"Money makes people do the strangest things," Mavis said. There was something unsettling about discussing these dark realities amidst the cosy embrace of books and stories.

"But there's something that doesn't add up,"

Gemma went on, her voice only just audible over the hum of the new point-of-sale system. "Dominic's medication — it's prescription only. So how did they get hold of it? Whoever it was, they couldn't have just picked it up at the corner shop."

Mavis nodded, her eyes narrowing in thought. "Dominic couldn't have been stockpiling it either. If he'd missed doses, he would've been ill long before. And everyone says he was fit as a fiddle right up until—"

"Until he wasn't," Gemma finished, the finality of the statement hanging between them.

The two women sat in silence, contemplating how their potential killer could have sourced the amount of propranolol that was found in Dominic's system.

"Sorry, I couldn't help but overhear..."

Jack's voice sliced through the air, startling both the women. He was looking up apologetically from the computer screen. Gemma and Mavis turned towards him.

"Oh Jack, we're just..." Gemma began, colouring in embarrassment at being caught in such a grotesque discussion amidst the Sunday quiet of her bookshop.

Jack raised his hand before she could manage an explanation. "It's actually very easy to get hold of medication without a prescription," he said. "Illegal, but easy."

Chapter Twenty-Three

Jack leaned back in his chair. "You'd be surprised how easy it is," he began, tapping a rhythm on the keyboard with his fingers. "Medicine, drugs, weapons, you name it. It's all out there for sale. And if you're clever about it, you can cover your tracks too."

"Can you show me how?" Gemma's voice was tremulous. What exactly was Jack talking about? "Without doing anything illegal, that is?"

"Oh, yes, sure. I mean, it's not a crime to just take a look," Jack said. He had a mischievous twinkle that suggested he enjoyed the slight edge of danger way too much. "It's only a problem if you actually buy the forbidden fruit. Let me just finish up the setup on this point-of-sale system, and then we'll take a look."

"Perfect timing for a coffee break," Mavis said,

always eminently practical. "And perhaps a slice of that Victoria sponge?"

"Are you trying to fatten me up with all this cake?" Gemma said with a laugh.

"Oh, my dear, this nation was built on tea and cake."

They shuffled off towards the café. In a few minutes, the invigorating smell of fresh coffee filled the shop, while Gemma set out some cups and plates. Mavis sliced the Victoria sponge she'd brought along, revealing layers of jam and buttercream, and placed the slices on the plates. With the tray laden, they returned to the front of the shop where Jack awaited them.

"Right, then," Jack said, gently twisting the new point-of-sale monitor towards them. The screen came to life as his fingers clacked on the keyboard. "Both of you are familiar with web browsers, I presume?"

Gemma stirred her coffee, her spoon tinkling against the side of her cup. "How old do you think I am, Jack?" She chuckled.

Mavis let out a hearty laugh, the lines around her eyes crinkling. "Even I know what a browser is!" she said, waving her fork in the air for emphasis.

"Good, good. Just checking," Jack responded with a smile.

With the screen turned towards the two women, he opened a program on the computer. Gemma thought it looked vaguely familiar.

"So, this is a web browser called Tor. It's what you use to access the dark web."

"Tor?" Gemma repeated, leaning forward. The 'dark web' was a term she'd frequently heard on TV. It sounded ominous and vaguely sinister. For some reason, it evoked an image of a spider lurking at the centre of its web. Gemma had never understood how, or indeed *why*, it worked.

"Tor is your gateway to the dark web. It's a bit like regular internet surfing, but it bounces your connection through a maze of servers and satellites. Makes it impossible to trace."

"Sounds like something out of James Bond," Mavis said with an air of mild bewilderment.

Jack gave a low chuckle. "Not far off, Mavis. Except, instead of a martini, we've got coffee and cake."

Gemma sipped her coffee and watched carefully. The Dark Web — a place where secrets were traded like currency, and people made unsavoury exchanges, hidden in the shadows of anonymity. It was fascinating and frightening all at once.

Jack brought up a webpage splashed with a cartoonish pirate flag. "Welcome to Black Beard's Emporium!" he announced.

"Black Beard?" Gemma snorted. Really, the name seemed more descriptive of a children's fast-food restaurant rather than a marketplace for contraband.

"Ah, be fooled by the name, ladies," Jack smiled.

"Comical though it may be, this place is the real deal." His fingers danced across the keyboard, and suddenly, rows upon rows of cannabis offerings came up on the screen. "See? Anything you want, just a few clicks away."

"Blimey!" Mavis muttered, leaning in closer to peer at the screen. Her eyes were remarkably sharp, despite her age. Nothing got past Mavis Rawlings, not even the prices of cannabis on the dark web.

Gemma sat silently, an array of conflicting emotions surging through her. "I didn't know it was this... accessible." Her voice conveyed disbelief, and slight disgust.

Jack looked at her. "Watch this."

He typed in 'hand gun' and hit enter. The screen refreshed, now showing glossy images of firearms with detailed descriptions.

"Guns?" Gemma's voice was almost a squeal. "But how do people get these delivered?"

"Ah," Mavis interjected with a feigned nonchalance, "I suppose one would skulk around in the park at midnight, waiting for a shadowy figure to approach one and trade the goods for cash."

"Nothing so dramatic, I'm afraid," Jack grinned. "It's actually much simpler. Your orders are just shipped through the post. Well, I don't know about guns — but drugs certainly are."

"In the post?" Gemma's apprehension was transformed into utter incredulity now. "Just like that? With the normal postal system?"

"Exactly, just like that." Jack nodded. "Put in the normal post, all very well packaged and nondescript. On the outside, they're just normal parcels. The seller's untraceable, so it's the buyer who takes the risk."

"Good heavens!" Gemma exclaimed, her mind reeling. Such dangerous transactions and illegal activities happening under the guise of the everyday mail? It was completely unheard of!

Gemma leaned back against the counter, her arms crossed over her chest, pondering this new information that Jack had just bestowed upon them.

"Wouldn't a dog sniff out the drugs?" Mavis asked sceptically. "Or one of those security machines detect them?" She was still half-inclined to think that Jack was playing a practical joke.

"They do have their ways of figuring it out, of course," he said, "but these folks are crafty. They wrap their wares multiple times in airtight packaging — and I mean really airtight. Then they'll sneak the contraband inside, say, a teddy bear or a box of breakfast cereal. Anything to disguise the real parcel and throw the authorities off the scent."

Gemma's eyes widened. The quaint post office, with its red-brick façade and its old pillar boxes, seemed far less innocent now. "And you've seen this happen? At the sorting office?"

"Once or twice," Jack confessed in a confidential whisper. "If a parcel's damaged and the contents are, well, suspicious, then we have to report it. But ninety-nine times out of a hundred, it passes through, right under our noses. It will be delivered like any other parcel."

"Remarkable," Gemma murmured, shaking her head. It was uncomfortable to think that most illicit items could pass through the postal system that way, completely undetected. Why, this was plain smuggling — and actually with the help of the post, no less!

Mavis glanced out at the marketplace visible through the bookshop's front window. She imagined all manner of contraband passing by, hidden in plain sight.

"So, this is where anyone could lay their hands on all sorts of prescription medicine," she said. "I suppose they'd look rather innocent among birthday cards and online shopping returns."

Jack straightened up. "That's correct. A bit of bubble wrap, a Jiffy bag, and Bob's your uncle. Just another package in the postie's bag, and no one the wiser."

Gemma glanced at Mavis, whose eyes mirrored her own feelings of curiosity and apprehension. "The wonders of technology, eh? We've definitely been living in the dark ages, Mavis," she said with a rueful smile.

"Or in blissful ignorance, perhaps," Mavis replied dryly.

The two women exchanged a look of wry understanding. Gemma drummed her fingers in a staccato rhythm on the countertop.

"Jack, could you look up propranolol? Just to see if it's available on there."

Jack looked up at Gemma. "Beta-blockers? Sure," he said, his fingers poised above the keyboard. "I'd be shocked if it wasn't available."

He typed in the name with a brisk, business-like clack, and navigated through the results.

In the next second, a list materialised on the screen, showing countless options for propranolol, in various quantities and dosages from different suppliers.

"Bingo!" Gemma exclaimed, grimly triumphant. The cogs in her sleuth's mind turned rapidly, piecing together a part of the puzzle. "This is how our killer could've got their hands on enough propranolol to be lethal!"

Jack raised an eyebrow. "Do I want to know what you ladies are cooking up?"

"It's probably best not to," said Gemma, giving a pat on his shoulder. "I've already said too much. But it's really interesting to see how easy it is to get hold of these things."

"Just as simple as buying a computer game online," Jack said. His voice was flat, almost as if illegal drug procurement was just another one of the banalities of life. "Stuff like this doesn't stick out at all in the post if it's packaged well."

Mavis, whose attention had been fixed to the screen again, turned suddenly to Jack.

"But surely, if this is all so clandestine, how do they pay for these things? Any payment could be traced back to your bank card, couldn't it?"

"Ah yes," Jack said with a smile. "That's where Bitcoin comes in."

"Bit... Coin?" Mavis was visibly bewildered. God only knew what infernal technological creation *this* was going to be!

"Never heard of it," Gemma admitted rather apologetically, feeling like she'd missed the memo on some crucial, obvious bit of modernity.

"Really?" Jack's eyes widened just a fraction. Then he gave a light chuckle. "Well, let's just say it's online money — much harder to trace than your bank cards."

Both women stared blankly at each other, and then at the young man in front of them. The very notion of cryptocurrency felt as alien to them as the surface of Mars. Jack reclined in his chair, preparing to unpack the mystery of bitcoin for Gemma and Mavis. The computer screen cast an almost otherworldly light on the trio as they sat huddled behind the counter of the cosy bookshop, surrounded by empty cups and plates.

"Think of it like setting up a digital wallet," Jack began, tapping away at the keyboard with a confidence that drew Gemma's envy. "Sort of like a bank account where you store bitcoins instead of pounds."

Gemma squinted at the screen, trying to locate this so-called wallet amidst the sea of unfamiliar terms and images. Mavis, too, looked perplexed. Her hand instinctively patted her actual purse, as if to reassure herself that wallets were still tangible things one could hold.

"Oh dear, it all sounds terribly complicated," Gemma murmured. She'd never been one to avoid technology, but she felt utterly out of her depths on this one.

"It's not, really," Jack said, giving them an encouraging grin. "It's actually no more complex than online banking." He glanced at Gemma, who still looked confused.

"Alright, imagine your regular bank account," he continued, using his hands to illustrate his point. "You can deposit money into it, right?"

"Of course," Mavis chimed in, nodding along.

"Now let's say you're travelling abroad. Then, you can go to the bank and exchange some of that money for another currency — say, Euros or US dollars."

"Done that plenty of times before," Gemma said, feeling a bit more confident now that they were treading familiar ground.

"It's the same idea with a Bitcoin exchange," Jack explained. "You put your money in, convert it to Bitcoin, and voila! You've got yourself some digital cash to spend in places like Black Beard's Emporium!"

"Sounds like an adventure novel," Mavis sighed. Her

mind was already conjuring up images of cyberspace pirates and treasure chests filled with electronic coins.

Everything finally clicked into place in Gemma's mind. "So, you swap your real money for this— this Bitcoin, and then you can buy anything on the dark web without it being traced back to you."

"Exactly!" Jack confirmed. With a click of the mouse, he brought up a colourful chart on the screen that represented the value of bitcoin. It looked more like a roller coaster to Gemma — one she wasn't sure she'd ever want to ever ride.

"Do you have any Bitcoin, Jack?" she asked.

"I have, a little bit. I dabbled in mining for coins a few years ago, but their value is too unstable to put any real money in."

"Mining?"

"You can get your computer to solve complex math puzzles to create new coins," Jack stated. Gemma gave him a bewildered stare. "Oh, but don't worry! You don't really need to know about all that. You can simply exchange pounds for Bitcoin."

Gemma heaved a sigh of relief. She didn't have it in her to go into mathematics of all things, right now.

Mavis leaned closer, her bewilderment now transformed into fascination. "Quite a world we live in!" she said, squinting at the screen. "So, let me see if I understand it properly. This Bitcoin malarkey is essentially just like normal money, then?"

"Similar," Jack replied, his fingers poised over the keyboard like a pianist ready to launch into a concerto. "Except that it's only digital. No actual coins or notes. And you can only use it to buy things on the dark web without leaving a paper trail."

"Dark web shopping," Gemma murmured, half to herself. It felt akin to ordering tea bags from the moon. "And how is this supposed to be more secure?"

"Alright, so," Jack began, tapping away at the keys to pull up another window, "when you pay with Bitcoin, your money goes through something called a tumbler." He turned to face them. "It's split up, bounced around different accounts to obscure its origin. That makes the transaction tough to trace."

"A bit like money laundering?"

"Sort of, yeah. Money laundering is taking illegal money and making it appear clean. Using a tumbler isn't illegal in itself, though. It just makes the money seem more anonymous by hiding where it comes from, whether it's illegal or legal."

A smile played on his lips. He leaned back, arms crossed, satisfied with his explanation. "You could say it's the modern way to buy nefarious goods without leaving a trail of breadcrumbs for the police to follow."

"Modern indeed!" Mavis huffed. "In my day, the closest thing we had to a tumbler was the washing machine. Or a whisky glass." She shook her head.

Gemma chuckled, picturing Mavis trying to stuff a

pile of illicit banknotes into her Hotpoint on the spin cycle. She turned to Jack, still slightly shocked at the discoveries of the morning.

"Well, that was very enlightening. And quite helpful. It might just explain how our killer could get their hands on prescription drugs, without leaving a paper trail. Jack, you've been a tremendous help."

Gemma gave the young man a grave smile. "But we must ask you to keep this between us. It's imperative that no one knows we're looking into the murder."

"Of course." Jack nodded. He wasn't just a postal worker or a part-time tech wizard anymore. He was now an accomplice of their amateur sleuthing — a secret keeper in their quest for justice.

"Right then," Mavis clapped her hands, determined to shake off the weight of their digital dive. "Shall we take a break for lunch? All this talk of tumblers and the dark web has made my stomach grumble louder than the church bells before a Sunday service."

"Even after all those cakes?" Gemma twinkled.

"Cakes are food for the mind, not the body, my dear."

"Touché!"

"After lunch, I'll show you both how to use the hand terminals for stocktaking." Jack grinned, looking forward to showing something far less nefarious than illegal marketplaces, and far more immediately useful.

"Inventory management," Mavis sighed, a bemused smile tugging at her lips. "Now, that's more my speed!"

Chapter Twenty-Four

Gemma was perched precariously behind the counter, on the edge of her usual stool, balancing a hefty tome on her thigh — *Bitcoin Explained*. She'd always prided herself on understanding at least a little bit of every subject that lined her shelves. But this... The more she read, the more confused she felt. It was like trying to decipher an ancient text in a long-forgotten language.

"Bitcoins... Blockchain... And *mining*..." she muttered to herself, exasperated. "They might as well be talking about fairy gold!"

It had all started with Jack's unsettling demonstration yesterday. Gemma had barely slept, grappling with the unnerving fact that any person could slip easily into the dark web's embrace and buy anything they wanted. Narcotics, weapons — and beta-blockers used to commit deliberate murder and make it look like an accidental overdose. The sheer simplicity of it all terrified her.

“Morning, Gemma! Fancy reading material you’ve got there!” Sarah said, cheerful as always, as she emerged from the café at the back.

Her white linen frock danced around her knees as she peered over the counter, her eyes landing on the open page bristling with graphs and technical jargon.

“Bitcoin, huh? I’ve heard it’s like riding a roller coaster without a seatbelt. Lots of ups and downs, and plenty of people take a serious tumble.”

Gemma closed the book with a snap and gave a resigned sigh.

“I’m just trying to wrap my head around it all,” she said, pushing the book aside. “It’s all rather perplexing, Sarah. Money, real enough, that you can’t see or touch. And now I’m reading that people mine it on their computers without so much as an axe, or a helmet. God only knows what’ll be next!”

Sarah offered a sympathetic smile. “I don’t think you need to worry too much about these new currencies. They’re just a fad, I’m sure. Our good old pound sterling isn’t going anywhere.”

Gemma gave a light chuckle, appreciating the sentiment. “I’ll keep that in mind. Thanks, Sarah!” Sarah’s fingers drummed lightly on the counter.

“Gemma, do you mind if I take next Friday off? It’s

my friend Jenny's 30th birthday. She's having a getaway of sorts in Newcastle, and I'd really like to go."

"Oh of course, Sarah," Gemma replied with a gentle smile. "Just make sure the rota is sorted, so we're not left in the lurch."

"Will do!" Sarah beamed. "I'll talk with the part-time staff and swap some shifts." She paused, a nostalgic grin spreading across her face. "We're going for a meal, and then hitting some bars and clubs later on. I'm really excited!"

"Sounds like a riot," Gemma commented, the corners of her mouth turning up at the memory of her own 30th — a night enveloped in a fog of endless laughter and one too many glasses of Rosé.

Before the conversation could wander further down memory lane, Mavis ambled towards them, the new stock system's hand terminal clutched in her hand.

"You know, this new-fangled thingamajig isn't half bad! All the romance novels are tallied up and tucked into the system. And I didn't press the wrong button once!"

"Thank you, Mavis," Gemma said, happy to see her friend's gleeful acceptance of the new point-of-sale system. She'd reckoned Mavis would run into some problems adjusting to the new technology, but it had been a pretty smooth transition so far.

Sarah took this as her cue to go back to the café to

rearrange the rota. Mavis eased onto the stool behind the counter.

"I've been thinking," Gemma whispered, thumbing through the book of cryptocurrency, "I should have a word with David about Dominic's case. It's probably time to involve the police. Now that we have an idea about how someone could have procured the drugs, we should at least put forth the idea of there being foul play in his death."

"Reckon he'll take to our theory?"

Gemma gave a determined nod. "He's sharp, Mavis. If something is amiss, he'll undoubtedly sniff it out. Convincing him to reopen the case is another thing, though. If it has already been closed, that is."

With a deep breath, Gemma pulled out her phone from her pocket. She tapped out a message, her fingers tentatively writing and then erasing a few times. Finally, she decided to just be straightforward.

"Can we meet tomorrow?" She texted David.

The reply came quickly, the ping from her phone cutting through the silence.

"For a drink in the evening?"

"Could I come to your office at the station instead?" Gemma countered, her heart skipping a beat as she adjusted her glasses and peered at the tiny text.

David's response was prompt, business-like. *"10am okay?"*

"Perfect, thanks." A small smile glowed on her face.

Gemma sent the message, and then placed her phone on the counter. Mavis leaned in, her eyes twinkling. She was an incurable romantic, and Gemma's history with David had captured her interest.

"Do you think David thought you were asking him out for a... *sociable* drink?"

"Probably," Gemma said with a shrug. She had to admit, the idea wasn't without its charm.

Mavis met Gemma's eyes. "That may not be such a bad thing, my dear. You know, if you still have feelings for him."

Gemma sighed. A lock of hair fell over her eye, and she brushed it away.

"I do still like him," she confessed, her gaze drifting to the books on a nearby shelf. "But I was the one who ended things, Mavis. And I ended them for a very good reason. Jumping back into anything... It just seems ill-advised. Especially when we're about to discuss a murder investigation."

"Ah, love." Mavis smiled. "Just give it some time."

Chapter Twenty-Five

Gemma hesitated for a moment before pushing open the heavy glass door to Ripley Police Station — a decision she'd debated ever since departing the Bookworm. Ripley was the nearest town to Belper, about seven miles north, and housed the district police headquarters.

The cold, white light of the police station entrance seemed to drain the warmth of the spring day Gemma had left behind, and the unmistakable scent of industrial cleaner hung in the air.

"Morning," she addressed the officer at the front desk, hoping her voice didn't betray her nervousness. "I'm here to see DI Haynes. We have an appointment for 10 a.m."

The officer, his hair a disciplined crop of grey, peered

at her through his thick, round glasses. Suddenly, there was a gleam of recognition in his eyes.

"Ah, Gemma! How're you doing? It's been a while since we've seen you here!"

"I'd like to say it's a social visit," Gemma said, smiling politely, "but I need to talk to David about something important."

"Of course." He turned to his computer. With a few clicks, he located her appointment and buzzed her through.

"You remember where you're going?"

"Sure do."

Gemma's heartbeat climbed up a notch. Reporting a suspected murder was hard enough. And she had to report it to her ex-fiancé! She had been determined to keep her distance ever since they broke up, regardless of her feelings. And now here she was at his very doorstep, with a fantastical half-baked theory of murder, no less.

Gemma's conviction suddenly vanished. What if she ended up looking crazy? What if David didn't believe her?

Trudging upstairs, she found herself in a sparse waiting area that boasted chairs about as comfortable as stone slabs. She'd barely taken in her surroundings when David emerged from his office.

"Gemma!" he said, his eyes lighting up with genuine pleasure.

He ushered her into his office, a room that looked

like it had weathered a paper mill explosion. The desk was covered in folders thrown about carelessly, and the whiteboards on each wall were splattered with multi-hued sticky notes. *That's what a real 'murder board' looks like*, Gemma told herself.

"Take a seat," David gestured, somewhat flustered as he cleared a stack of folders off a chair. Gemma perched on the edge, taking in David's features. Time, and perhaps one too many pub lunches, had filled him out. His shirt strained across his waist, and his cheeks had lost their once-prominent bone structure. She kept her observations to herself — this wasn't the time or the place to get personal.

"Sorry about the mess," he said, following her gaze. "Occupational hazard." He didn't sound apologetic at all.

Gemma twisted a bracelet on her wrist, a childhood nervous tic that she'd never quite managed to shake. She cleared her throat.

"I'm here about a potential murder case," she announced, her voice steady despite the butterflies fluttering in her stomach.

David's reaction was immediate. His eyes shone with mirth, and his lips twisted into a smug grin. "Ironic!" He said. "You leave me because my job takes up all my time, and now here you are, knocking at my door to increase my caseload."

"Yes, well, the irony isn't lost on me," Gemma

replied, fighting the flush that threatened to climb her neck. She'd never enjoyed having her contradictions pointed out, especially not by David.

Sensing her discomfort, David coughed into his hand. Gemma knew him well enough to understand that he was about to switch gears.

"So, what's this about then?" His voice was brisk and business-like.

"It's Dominic Westley," Gemma said gravely. "The writer."

"Ah yes, I heard about that incident." David leaned forward, tapping into his keyboard. "He collapsed in your shop, didn't he?"

Gemma nodded, watching as David's fingers danced across the keys, searching for the police file on Dominic's demise.

"Pathology report states death by an overdose of propranolol beta blockers," he said, scanning the file with a frown. His voice was flat, as if reciting a shopping list. "Ruled an accidental death." He glanced up at Gemma.

"Dominic's flask — found in your bookshop, sent for analysis — just had coffee in it. The case was closed. Body released to the family for burial." He paused for a moment, tilting his head. "Are you suggesting this verdict might be off the mark?"

Gemma met his gaze, her eyes shining with conviction. "I firmly believe it is," she said. Her voice was steady as ever. The butterflies of a moment ago had all but vanished.

"Alright. And why do you think so?" David leaned back in his chair, which creaked at the sudden movement.

"Three principal persons of interest," Gemma began.

David smiled. "Looks like some of my job rubbed off on you after all."

"Hard not to pick up a thing or two," she replied. "Donna Westley, Ellie Simpson, and Geoff Dunsworth."

At the mention of Geoff, David's demeanour changed. His indulgent smile transformed into a grim look of recognition. "Geoff Dunsworth, huh? I'm well aware of his past."

Gemma hesitated, her words tumbling over one another like puzzle pieces that she didn't want to lay down.

"It was Donna who first voiced suspicions of foul play," she continued. "Despite their rocky past, she and Dominic were patching things up. She was supposed to move back in, the weekend after... after the incident."

A frown of concentration appeared on David's face as he prepared to take notes. "Reconciliation? That doesn't give her much of a motive, does it?" he said, holding his pen over the notepad.

"True, but there's more to it. Donna is convinced that Ellie Simpson was the other woman — the one

Dominic cheated on her with," Gemma paused, recalling Donna Westley's tear-stained face as she wrestled with grief and betrayal. "But I know for a fact that Dominic and Donna had already ended things before Ellie came into the picture. So, Ellie wasn't the other woman. Technically, I mean."

"But technicalities don't always soothe the wounded heart, eh?" David remarked, his pen scratching on his notepad.

"Perhaps not. I must mention, though, Donna seems to have a solid alibi. She was in York for the days leading up to Dominic's death."

"York, you say?"

"Yes, she spent an evening at an Indian restaurant there, and didn't return until the day after. So it seems unlikely that she could have been involved," Gemma explained, watching as David scribbled lines that apparently only he could decipher.

"Alibis can be verified, or they can crumble under scrutiny," he said, tapping the pen against his lips. "Anyone vouch for her presence in York?"

"She said she was there for a friend's birthday."

Gemma watched as David nodded absently. She knew he was rapidly thinking of ways to check the validity of Donna's claims.

"Easy enough to verify," David said, finishing his rapid note-taking. "Alright, what else have we got?"

Gemma shifted in the rigid chair opposite David's

cluttered desk, her fingers tracing the edge of a coffee-stained coaster. "I went to Dominic's house after he... passed," she continued, watching David's eyebrows rise.

"You did what?" His voice was sharp. "Gemma, you can't just waltz into a potential crime scene!"

"Wasn't exactly waltzing," Gemma retorted. "And it wasn't exactly a 'crime scene' to our knowledge at the time. Donna was visiting the house and asked me to go with her — she couldn't face it alone. She was due to move back into the house before Dominic passed, so she had the key."

"And?" David leaned over the desk, his features still set in a frown.

"The kitchen— it reeked of bleach. Donna said he was never the type to bleach a kitchen, or even hire a cleaner. Plus, it seems pretty strange behaviour to clean that deep when you're planning on overdosing on your medication."

"Unless it was an accidental overdose?" David pointed out, drumming his fingers absently on the desk. "But it does seem odd. That could be someone covering up evidence, but if his house was indeed the scene of a crime, it's compromised now."

He sighed, shaking his head at the muddied waters they now had to navigate.

"Speaking of odd," Gemma said, "Donna's finances haven't been great lately. Her coaching business is floundering, and—" she paused for dramatic effect, ensuring she had David's full attention, "Dominic was far from the successful writer everyone believed."

"Go on," David prompted, his faint humming conveying that he was piecing together the implications in his head.

"His bank statements were a shocker to Donna. She opened them while we were there," Gemma said. "Mountains of debt, no new royalties coming in. It seems his literary ship had sailed, and there was no gold to speak of."

David scribbled furiously, the pen almost burrowing through the paper.

"So," he said, the word hanging between them like a verdict, "Donna had a potential financial motive to patch things up with Dominic. Get back into the good graces of an ostensibly successful husband? But what you're saying is, Donna didn't realise he was in debt?"

"Exactly." Gemma felt a twinge of satisfaction at the sight of David's methodical mind turning over their theory. "Money has a way of complicating reconciliations, doesn't it?"

"Complicates everything."

Gemma shifted in her chair, gathering her thoughts. "There's also the matter of someone entering the house the morning after Dominic's death," she said, her voice steady. "Donna couldn't account for the alarm fob that was used."

"She didn't know who owned that fob?"

Gemma shook her head. "Dominic's neighbour saw a young lad in a black hoodie leaving the house the morning after his death. The time corresponds with the exit time in the alarm log. Couldn't see his face, though. And I spotted someone similar lurking at the back in Dominic's funeral." She watched as David's hand glided across the paper, his notes becoming more fervent with each revelation.

"Very suspicious," he muttered when he was done. "An unknown person entering the house, cleaning up evidence after the fact. That's something that should absolutely not be overlooked."

"Exactly my point," Gemma stated. Then she delved into the next piece of the puzzle. "Then there's Geoff Dunsworth, the builder."

"Ah, Geoff," David uttered in an almost singsong voice.

"Dominic owed Geoff a lot of money for the new kitchen and extension he built."

Gemma paused to let David catch up with his note taking. "Geoff stormed into Dominic's place while I was there with Donna. He was red-faced, all but frothing at the mouth. Claimed Dominic owed him thirty-grand. He was rather... emphatic about it."

"Emphatic?"

"Well, *threatening* might be more specific," Gemma said. "He was belligerent, yelling in Donna's face, he just wanted his money. And when he mentioned that the debt was now Donna's problem... well, you should have seen her. She turned white and started shaking like a leaf."

"He is known to have a raging temper."

"Yes, well, he made it quite clear that he expected Donna to cough up the money, which only adds another layer of complexity to the whole affair. Gave her a week to pay up."

"Layers upon layers," David mused, tapping the notepad with the end of his pen. "Looks like we're peeling an onion here, Gemma. And every layer has its own sting."

His pen danced across the page. "So, Donna had a potential motive for financial security," he muttered, skimming his notes, "access to the house, and means to tamper with his medicine. But she has an alibi."

After receiving a nod of confirmation from Gemma, he continued. "And Geoff Dunsworth — motivated by the outstanding debt, potential access to the property, and a history of violence."

"Right," Gemma sighed, folding her arms as she leaned back in her chair. David capped the pen with an authoritative click, and looked up at her.

"Now then, who's your third suspect?"

"Ellie Simpson," she said, scooting forward in her chair. Her fingertips drummed on the armrests. "She and Dominic were together for a while."

"Ah," David exhaled. He uncapped his pen once more.

"Donna marked her as the mistress, but Dominic was flying solo when Ellie entered the picture. At least, that's what he told her. And that's what she told me."

Gemma's eyes rested on the way David's handwriting sloped across the notepad. His scrawl was as incomprehensible as ever.

"As for who Dominic actually cheated on Donna with — well, that's still a mystery to me."

David scribbled another note, the corners of his mouth twitching upwards momentarily. Gemma cleared her throat.

"Ellie and Dominic," she began, "evidently broke up not long before... Well, before he died. Turns out Ellie was pregnant, and Dominic didn't exactly embrace impending fatherhood. Turned her out of the house."

David's face was grave. "He wanted her to get rid of the baby?"

"Adamantly, from what I've gathered." Gemma's voice softened. "But Ellie stood her ground. Refused to terminate the pregnancy. She's just about five months pregnant right now."

"That's rough," David whistled, the pen pausing on his pad. "So, we're looking at a motive of revenge? For being spurned and pressured? It isn't the happiest of love stories, is it?"

"Perhaps," Gemma said with a small frown. "But

Ellie... I don't see her resorting to murder over it." Her voice conveyed a staunch conviction. "After all, what would murdering him accomplish? Only that her baby would remain fatherless forever."

"Fair point. But her alibi will need verifying regardless. Emotions can drive people to extremes."

"Of course," Gemma said, watching as David scribbled something indecipherable onto the paper.

"What about the medicine? Propranolol, wasn't it? It was his own, leading to the accidental overdose verdict."

"Both Donna and Ellie were aware of Dominic's condition," Gemma pointed out. "Donna showed me everything after he passed — boxes of medication, nothing missing, no extras. It's prescription-only. You can't just hoard it like paracetamol. And he couldn't have hoarded the amount found in his system without becoming seriously ill. Or forging prescriptions."

"The medicine's restricted, but not unobtainable," David interjected.

Gemma nodded.

"Still," David went on, his gaze shifting back to his notes, "it's a lead that must be explored." The pen resumed its dance across the paper as he jotted down another line, every fact and hunch documented meticulously.

Gemma watched him work in silence. His focused eyes, and that familiar frown of concentration tugged at memories that were better left undisturbed. She rested her hands on the desk.

"I've been thinking," she began, her voice measured, "about how someone could've got their hands on propranolol without a prescription."

David set his pen down. "And what's your theory?"

She hesitated for a moment, then pushed ahead. "The dark web. It's unnervingly easy to find this stuff on there."

"Ah, yes," David sighed, "digital black markets. They make our lives very difficult here." His tone was one of weary resignation. He scrawled a few more words on his notepad, and then simply sat there, his eyes fixed on the ceiling and his fingertips pressed together.

Gemma's voice cut through the stillness, a desperate urgency woven in her words. "David, do you think we have a case?"

David weighed her question for a few moments.

"It's worth pursuing," he said finally. The detective within him was intrigued — he would be truly remiss to ignore the trail she had uncovered. "We can't just haul people in for questioning, though."

"Then what's the next step?" Gemma asked, her eyes sparkling with excitement.

"We'll start by having uniformed officers chat with everyone involved. Making routine enquiries." He turned back to his computer, and pulled up records with a few deft clicks. "It says here you were interviewed by an officer?"

"Yes. Sergeant Nicholls and PC Smith came to the Bookworm, the day after Dominic died."

"Right," David said, tapping the keyboard. "Let's see where this leads us." His voice was resolute, the click of the keyboard punctuating his commitment to unravelling the mystery.

"Officers will pay another visit to your shop. They'll need to speak to everyone present on the day of his death."

Gemma nodded. "That will be Mavis, my shop assistant, and Sarah, who runs the café."

"Good. We'll also need to have a chat with Ellie, Donna, and Geoff." His fingers paused over the keyboard. "Get their versions of what happened."

A frown flickered across his face. Regardless of Gemma's conviction, David was only too aware that they didn't actually have any proof. The case against all three 'persons of interest' was still purely conjecture.

"And you'll take it forward from there, right?" Gemma interrupted his ruminations.

"Yes, I'll get right on it." He reached for his desk phone to make the arrangements.

"Thank you, David, for looking into this."

David leaned back in his chair, which gave another pitiful creak. "It's my job, Gemma. Besides, when new information comes to light, we investigate — that's how it works."

A mischievous smirk played on his lips. "I must admit, though, when you rang me, I'd hoped it was to ask me for a drink. A murder investigation isn't exactly what I had in mind."

Gemma responded with a smile. Her eyes conveyed a mixture of amusement and nostalgia, a silent acknowledgment of their shared past. "Well, I never said the two had to be mutually exclusive."

The laugh that followed was genuine, but tinged with disappointment. "Now that you're embroiled in a potential murder case, that would be quite the conflict of interest," he said with mock solemnity. "But perhaps, once all this is sorted out..."

"Then it's a date," Gemma finished, the words light and teasing, even as she pondered the future conversations that might unfold in a less official setting, bolstered by liquid courage.

Chapter Twenty-Six

The familiar peal of the bell reassured Gemma as she opened the door of the Bookworm. She hung her coat wearily on the rack, and settled behind the counter for what she prayed would be an afternoon of just selling books. She had no energy for anything else.

Mavis disentangled herself from a new shipment of poetry books and came towards her, peering over her glasses with an inquisitive glint in her eyes. "Everything go well at the station?"

Gemma offered a nod. "Yes, it went well," she said. "David said he'll be sending uniforms over to take statements, including yours, mine, and Sarah's." She absently scanned a customer's purchase. "He also said they'll need to speak to Donna, Ellie, and Geoff."

"Hopefully, that'll be enough for them to figure this whole mess out."

Gemma allowed herself a small smile as she handed the customer their change. Mavis walked back to the pile of poetry books and resumed her dusting.

About an hour later, two unfamiliar uniformed officers stepped into the quiet confines of the Bookworm.

"Good afternoon," one said, his voice carrying the unmistakable authority of the law. "I'm Constable Kent, and this is Constable Laine. Are Mavis Rawlings and Sarah Hastings working today?"

"Certainly, Constable. Mavis is over by those shelves," Gemma said, pointing, "and Sarah is working in the café at the back of the shop."

"We would like to talk to them," said Constable Kent. "Please."

"Of course." Gemma stifled the flutter of curiosity in her chest. "Do you need to speak with me again?"

"No, we have your statement, recorded by DI Haynes," Constable Kent assured her. His eyes scanned the room until they landed on Mavis, who had emerged from the poetry section.

"Hello, I'm Mavis Rawlings," she politely addressed the police officers. "Pleased to meet you."

"Good morning. I'm Constable Kent. We'd be grateful for a moment of your time, Mrs. Rawlings. We'd like to ask you some questions."

"Of course."

"Right. This way, please. You can use my office." Gemma gestured towards the back office, a small, cluttered space that housed more than its fair share of forgotten tales and dusty ledgers.

Mavis gave Gemma an encouraging nod and followed the police without hesitation. Gemma watched them disappear into the back office. She turned her attention back to the remaining customers.

Sarah strolled over to the counter where Gemma was stacking a display of local interest books, glancing at the officers with a hint of alarm. Her dress, a splash of bright florals against the muted background of the shop, seemed to ripple with her uneasy movements.

"Everything okay, Gemma?" Sarah's voice wavered, her gaze flitting towards the closed door of the back office.

"Oh, yes. Routine enquiries," Gemma assured her, with a small smile that she hoped would convey a sense of normalcy. "They're looking into the events surrounding Dominic's death. And since you were working the day, he— well, you know — they'll want to have a quick word with you too."

"Me?" Sarah's eyes widened. She bit her lip nervously. "I suppose that makes sense," she said finally, putting up a brave front.

"Nothing to worry about," Gemma said lightly. "It's just standard procedure." She watched as Sarah nodded, her shoulders relaxing as she disappeared back into the café.

After about thirty minutes, Mavis emerged from the back office, as composed as ever. She retrieved her duster from the counter, and began carefully dusting the history books.

"Mavis!" Gemma's voice was a confidential whisper. "How'd it go?"

"Much as expected," Mavis responded, her eyes focused on the dusting. "They wanted to confirm the sequence of events on the day Dominic graced us with his presence. They mostly asked me about when I invited him, and what time he arrived, and so on."

"Right," Gemma said. Before she could probe further, Constable Kent reappeared. He looked around at the café, and then signalled for Sarah to join them in the back office.

"You'll be fine. They're just trying to understand about our book signing event, and what led up to Dominic collapsing," Gemma called out after Sarah, who offered a tentative smile over her shoulder before following the officers.

Mavis leaned in closer to the counter. "Are they going to see Donna, Ellie, and Geoff next? What do you think they'll ask them?"

"David said they would," Gemma replied. "But I know nothing beyond that. It's all in the hands of the police now."

The next half hour ticked by slowly, and a steady stream of customers entered the shop, greeted by the soft chime of the bell. Gemma tapped away at the new point-of-sale system, still in awe at its sleek screen and satisfying beeps, and how quick they made the billing process. Mavis flitted between the sections, chatting with customers, recommending books, and keeping the shelves neat and tidy.

A few minutes later, the door of the back office opened quietly. Sarah emerged, looking pale, her usually bright eyes clouded with worry. Her hands trembled slightly as she smoothed the fabric of her dress.

"Thank you for your cooperation," Constable Kent said, tipping his hat with the polite detachment that is distinctive of English bobbies.

"Of course, anytime," Gemma said with a practiced smile, her eyes following their departure through the bookshop window.

Once the police car had left, she approached Sarah. Her voice conveyed a gentle solicitude. "Are you alright, Sarah?"

Sarah hesitated. "Yes, it was just... it was a lot," she gulped. "I'm not used to being questioned like that."

"Can I ask what they wanted to know?" Gemma's inquiry was gentle, but firm.

"They asked if I knew Dominic, or if I knew anything about his health." Sarah's reply was accompanied with a frantic shake of the head. "I told them I knew of him, of course. Everyone does, after all. But I didn't know him personally, and I had no idea he had a heart condition."

"Anything else?"

Sarah sighed. "Just general questions, really. About my job here, where I live... all that sort of thing. Although what that has to do with Dominic's accident, I don't know." She let out a deep breath, as if trying to shake off the weight of the interrogation, and her shoulders rose and fell.

Gemma gave her a reassuring smile. "Sounds like standard procedure, Sarah. Nothing to fret about."

"Thanks, Gemma." Sarah smiled, a ghost of her usual warmth returning to her face. She was dabbing her forehead with a napkin, still quivering all over.

"Really, it didn't sound so bad, my dear," Mavis ventured, anxious to reassure the young woman.

"Bad? Oh, no, I suppose not!" Sarah's voice shook. "I'm just— well, you know, I'm just a nervous person."

"It's just normal police enquiries, my dear," Mavis said warmly, her voice like a blanket enveloping the chilly room. "They asked me the same questions when it was my turn. They have to get a full account from the witnesses, you know. Just as a formality."

Sarah smiled, slightly abashed. "I suppose you're right. I'm sorry. Anxiety can really get the better of me sometimes."

"There, there," Mavis said. She put a hand on Sarah's arm, and gave it a reassuring squeeze.

With a smile, Sarah patted the older woman's hand and quickly retreated to the café. The next minute, the clinking of cups and the hum of the espresso machine signalled her welcome return to routine.

Once she was out of earshot, Mavis gave a sympathetic cluck. "Sarah really didn't take the questioning well, did she?"

"No. She looked white as a mouse. But well, she is quite an anxious person at the best of times. Being put on the spot about anything is bound to feel unnerving," Gemma said with a shrug, "let alone being questioned by two burly policemen."

"Poor thing," Mavis nodded. "I guess they'll be off to see Donna, Ellie, and Geoff next, won't they? How long do you think the questioning will take?"

"God only knows," Gemma said. She busied herself with straightening a stack of books on the counter, her fingers lingering on the spines.

"David did say he'd try to get to the bottom of this as soon as possible. It's all in their hands now."

Chapter Twenty-Seven

Gemma was busy organising the latest shipment of books at the Bookworm. The morning was a sunny, pleasant one, with a cool breeze blowing through the trees and meadows of Belper. A few stray, white clouds scurried in the sky, giving the quaint town the aspect of a latter-day pastoral idyll.

Gemma was in a great mood. She placed each new book onto the polished shelves, humming a quiet tune. The pleasant monotony of her task allowed her mind to wander. Involving the police into their murder investigation had lifted a weight off her shoulders. Now, it was all up to them. And if she was being honest, meeting David again had truly been a delight.

Gemma scanned the books one by one with the point-of-sale terminal, smiling to herself. As she reached into another cardboard box, something caught her attention. Her fingers brushed against the glossy cover of *Paper Boats in the Monsoon* – fifteen copies, all brand new.

Gemma paused, holding a copy aloft. It was a beautiful hardcover, its title embossed in elegant gold lettering, the cover a lively picture of a monsoon landscape. Its very vibrance seemed ironic, in light of the tragedy it now represented.

As Gemma flipped through the crisp pages, she felt a sense of melancholy creeping in. Dominic Westley, the local literary genius turned murder victim, had been far from a saint, with his pompous air and his wandering eye. But an untimely death was a judgement he hadn't deserved — let alone one brought about by a human hand.

The tinkle of the door's bell shattered Gemma's thoughts. To her surprise, it was Donna.

"Got a minute, Gemma?" she asked, nervously wringing her hands. It was more of a plea than a question, her voice trembling with urgency. She sounded almost *desperate*.

"Of course!" Gemma set down Dominic's book with a soft thud. They made their way to the back of the bookshop, and sat in the corner furthest away from the counter.

"Sarah, could we get a couple of coffees over here,

please?" Gemma called out. Sarah flashed a quick smile before bustling about to prepare their order.

When two steaming cappuccinos were set down in front of them, Gemma leaned forward. The relative privacy of their corner, punctuated by the muted sounds of page-turning and the occasional clink of porcelain, allowed her to carefully assess Donna. The woman had a troubled frown on her face, and her entire demeanour spelt one thing: fear.

"What's wrong?"

Donna's eyes darted left and right, as if expecting the bookshelves themselves to be eavesdropping.

"The police came by to ask me questions," she began, her fingers tracing the rim of her cup. "And I met them at Dominic's house."

"Concerning Dominic?" Gemma prodded. "They came here to talk to Mavis, Sarah, and me too."

"Yes. I told them my theories about Ellie. About how she could— she could be guilty." Donna's voice was steady, but her frantically knotting hands betrayed her anxiety. "And I mentioned how the kitchen reeked of bleach, you remember? Like a hospital ward after a health scare."

"I mentioned that to them too. What did they say?" Gemma leaned in, curiosity overshadowing her concern.

"Not much," Donna shrugged. "They said the crime scene was compromised, which is hardly a surprise. They're sending a team to check for fingerprints."

"Compromised?" Gemma echoed.

Donna nodded. "But there's more." She reached into her handbag, and pulled out a small notepad filled with meticulous notes. "Dominic was very particular about his paperwork. Always kept copies of the prescriptions." Donna thumbed through the pages, stopping at one lined with dates and dosages. "I showed this to the police. We checked his medicine box together. All the propranolol, for his heart, was accounted for. They don't think he was misusing it. Well, not on first inspection." Donna closed the notepad with a soft snap. "If only he'd applied the same precision to his relationships," she said with a deep sigh.

"Would have saved a lot of trouble," Gemma said wryly.

Donna's voice was barely audible above the hum of the bookshop. "I took them upstairs," she whispered, looking around nervously to ensure no one else was within earshot. "And in Dominic's ensuite... Gemma, I — I found something."

Gemma's eyes widened. "What did you find?"

"A used condom," Donna whispered, her face white with disgust. "In the bin. And it wasn't— it wasn't from me, Gemma. We hadn't— you know, since we agreed to give the relationship another shot."

The gasp that escaped Gemma could have rattled the teacups on their saucers. "They took it then? To test?" She clamped her mouth shut.

"Yes," Donna said, nodding solemnly. "They bagged it. It's evidence now."

A sudden crash behind the counter interrupted this tense conversation. Both women snapped their heads towards the source of the sound to see Sarah, her cheeks flushed red with embarrassment, gathering the pieces of a broken cup and saucer. Apologetic murmurs drifted over from nearby patrons as Sarah scrambled to clean up the mess.

"Sorry! So clumsy of me!" she called out, forcing a bright smile.

When the sympathetic clucks had finally ceased, and Sarah's blush had subsided into her usual rosy glow, Donna resumed.

"Once they run a DNA test..." she paused, eyeing Gemma with a meaningful glance. "It'll be interesting, won't it?"

"Ellie?" Gemma ventured. She knew it was what Donna wanted to hear. And she did not wish to correct her assumption that Ellie was the reason her marriage ended.

"Who else?" Donna spat. "Dominic never could resist her, even after everything!"

Gemma nodded, her mind already racing ahead to the implications of this new evidence. If the police narrowed down on a suspect, a DNA match would help clinch matters decisively. It would finally be a piece of concrete evidence.

"Those results could answer a lot of questions."

"Let's hope so," Donna sighed.

Gemma twirled a lock of hair around her finger. "So, what else did the police say?"

"Well, I had to give them my entire schedule, up until the day Dominic passed," Donna replied, ticking the days off on her fingers. "They asked all the details. I was in York, went for a curry. Even had to tell them I stopped at that service station off the M1 on the drive back."

"And you think they'll check up on all that?"

"I expect they will. That's the point, I suppose," Donna responded with a nonchalant shrug. "But that's alright. I'm not worried about that. I have nothing to hide."

Gemma nodded, taking a sip of her coffee. "Did they ask about anything else?"

Donna's face darkened, and her pleasant features transformed into a frown.

"Yes, they did. It felt— it was really intrusive, Gemma. They wanted to know about my business and finances. Or rather, the lack thereof. It sounded as if they were digging for a motive!"

She hugged herself tightly. "My finances are a mess, Gemma. And I didn't know how bad things were with Dominic's, either. It looks suspicious, doesn't it?"

Gemma reached across the table, offering a hand that was both steady and reassuring. "Don't fret too much, Donna. They're just being thorough. It's their job. And like you said, you've got nothing to hide, right?"

Donna gave her a small, grateful smile. "Thank you, Gemma."

The two women shared a moment of silence, letting the bustle of the café drown out their own thoughts and worries. The loud clatter of two empty coffee cups startled them out of their respective contemplations. Gemma seized the moment to broach another delicate subject.

"Donna, did you tell them about Geoff Dunsworth?"

Donna tensed. "Yes. Well, I mentioned it." She shivered despite the warmth of the spring afternoon. "I told them how threatening he was when he came around last week, demanding payment. I said it was rather scary, actually. I asked if I was responsible for Dominic's debt because we are still married. Were married, I mean, you know..."

"What did they say to that?"

"They said they couldn't comment on that." Donna looked crestfallen.

"I expect they'll want to speak to him too, then," said Gemma. "Being that demanding right after Dominic's death is definitely a little suspicious. No courtesy or compassion at all. Who does that?"

"They did tell me that they'd speak to him..."

The two women slowly finished their coffee. At length, Donna glanced at her watch, and rose from her chair, smoothing the fabric of her skirt.

"Thanks for listening, Gemma. It helps to talk about it."

"Anytime. You know where to find me." Gemma ushered her towards the door with a kind pat on the back.

"You've been a great friend, Gemma," Donna squeezed her hand, her eyes filled with gratitude. Gemma smiled.

These words evoked a sharp stab of guilt. She'd reported this woman, her *friend*, to David as a potential suspect.

Chapter Twenty-Eight

As the hands of the clock inched towards closing time on the next Thursday, the last customers left the store. And a few minutes later, the members of St. Mary's Chess Club trickled into the Bookworm. It was their weekly game evening, the first at the bookshop.

A motley crew of dedicated strategists shuffled through the door at the stroke of half past seven, chess boards in hand.

"Good evening, Gemma! I'm Henry," said a bespectacled man with a trimmed flaxen beard. His quiet authority clearly designated him the Club President.

"Good evening, Henry!" Gemma said brightly, leading the group to the café, where tables awaited them to set up their games. Sarah was manning her usual post behind the café counter, neatly arranging cups and saucers.

Gemma shot her a grateful smile. "Thanks for staying back to help, Sarah!"

"Happy to help!" the waitress called out. "Remember, I'm off tomorrow, though."

"Yes, I remember. It's your Newcastle trip, isn't it? Hope you have a great time!"

More chess aficionados filed in, and soon enough, the café buzzed with the ticks of the game timers, and the soft clicks of pieces settling into their squares. Gemma walked around, attending to the members and perusing the games. She paused behind a pair locked in the early stages of a Sicilian opening, transfixed. The knights danced forward, and their silent tango increased the tension.

"Ah, the Sicilian! A feisty choice," she remarked, her gaze following the pawns and the bishops vying for control.

"Do you play?" Roger turned to her. He was one of the club regulars, his strategic acumen matched only by the bushy luxuriance of his moustache.

"I used to quite a bit, at university," Gemma confessed, slightly sheepish. "But it's been ages since I've had a proper game."

"Care to sharpen those old skills?"

"Perhaps I will," Gemma said, smiling at the challenge. "Just be ready for a fight!"

Roger laughed good-humouredly. Just then, the bell above the door jangled violently. The door crashed open with such force that even the chess clocks seemed to pause their relentless ticking.

Gemma looked up in alarm. Framed in the doorway, his face crimson and his eyes ablaze with fury, stood the redoubtable Geoff Dunsworth.

"Need to talk!" he barked, his eyes darting around the room.

Gemma's first instinct was to protect the tranquillity of her bookshop-turned-chess-arena. "Let's not disturb the players," she said, motioning him to the back office.

Mavis, who had volunteered to stay late, stood behind the counter, carefully watching this exchange unfold. She followed without a word.

Once away from the pleasant quietude of the café, Geoff rounded on Gemma, his hands clenched tightly at his sides.

"Did you report me to the police?" he growled. "Or was it Donna?"

Gemma met his gaze calmly, even as waves of shock ran through her. "Why would you think I've spoken to them?"

"Because it's either you or Donna, isn't it?" Geoff hissed. "Why stir the pot, huh?"

"Mr Dunsworth," Gemma began, polite but icy, "the police are following up on Dominic's unexpected passing." She busily organised a stack of papers on her desk that didn't really need organising. "They have also questioned myself, Mavis, and Sarah from our café. If you're innocent, then I'm sure you've got nothing to worry about."

"Innocent?" Geoff's voice rose, desperate and pleading. "I haven't done a thing! But I'm stretched thin, Gemma! The money he owed me... it's for my crew, for their wages!"

Gemma looked up from her desk. She considered him for a moment — his weary face, the creases of worry on his forehead, the way his eyes searched hers for some semblance of understanding. Then she remembered Donna's pallor, the tremble in her voice, and the tears after their unsettling encounter.

"Geoff," she proceeded cautiously, "your visit to Dominic's was rather... intense. You terrified Donna, and you threatened her. So yes, I did mention it to the police. They asked me if I was aware of anyone who might have a reason to harm Dominic, anyone who might have threatened him. What did you expect me to say? Donna's so shaken by your demands, she refuses to be alone in that house now!"

Geoff looked as if someone had kicked the floor from under his feet. His face crumpled, and he collapsed into a chair, hands cradling his face like a child hiding from nightmares.

"I never meant to scare anyone!" he mumbled. His belligerent exterior revealed a man crumbling under pressure.

Mavis, who had listened silently to this outburst, left the room. "I'll be back in a moment."

Gemma looked at Geoff Dunsworth, the man who built walls for a living, now choking behind a wall of his own making. Deep in her heart, she felt a faint echo of sympathy for him.

"I'm sorry, Gemma!" Geoff's voice was a hoarse whisper, strained with remorse. "I was out of line. I didn't mean to give you or Donna a fright, I swear! I honestly just wanted my money. I *need* it!"

He lifted his head, his eyes glassy. "The coppers have me down as a suspect on account of the money Dominic owed. Asked if I knew about any health troubles he had. But I didn't have a clue about his health or his medicines!"

Gemma silently watched this sorry spectacle, the burly builder reduced to a bundle of nerves. It was clear the situation weighed heavily on him. His rugged face was painted in shades of fear.

Mavis breezed back into the room. Her hands cradled a steaming cup, which she placed before Geoff.

"Here, love. Drink this. Tea can mend more than you think," she said, beaming at the builder. Then, she pulled up a chair and sat beside Gemma, determined to radiate comfort and reassurance.

Geoff blinked at the two women, surprised at this sudden kindness. "Thanks," he grunted, wrapping his fingers around the warm cup.

Gemma bent forward, elbows on the desk. "Donna's planning on selling the house," she began, choosing her words carefully, "and she intends to settle all of Dominic's debts. I'm sure that will include yours too."

The builder gave a slow, tentative nod of relief. "I didn't know that, truly. And I'm— I'm sorry for barging in here like a bull in a china shop."

"Water under the bridge," Gemma replied with a small smile.

"Right," Geoff said, setting the cup down with a gentle clink. "I best be off. Got walls to build and all that. But thanks for the tea, ladies." He managed a grateful grin.

"Geoff, before you go, may I ask you something?" Gemma interjected, suddenly remembering something important.

"Certainly."

"Do you employ a young man, late teens maybe, who's partial to wearing large hoodies?"

A chuckle rumbled from Geoff's chest. "Most teenagers are hidden under their hoodies these days, aren't they? But yes, I do have an apprentice. Young lad named Ricky. Attends Derby College for construction studies. He helps me part-time."

"Ah, I see," Gemma said with a nod. "It's just that

Dominic's neighbour mentioned seeing a young boy in a hoodie leaving Dominic's house the morning after... he passed. Could it be one of your staff?"

"Ricky?" Geoff's brow furrowed. It was clear the thought had never crossed his mind. "I doubt it. Ricky didn't lay a single brick on Dominic's extension. He's been with another crew all the while, doing garden walls and block paving. Anyway, he only started working for me after the main construction on the extension was completed."

"Right, thanks, Geoff." Gemma sighed, in relief as much as disappointment. The lead might have gone cold, but every detail mattered. She gave Geoff a small, grateful smile. "That's good to know."

Geoff rose. "I'll keep you posted if I hear anything else from the coppers," he promised, his voice rough, but polite.

"Thanks, that would be really helpful," Gemma smiled.

With a nod more to himself than to them, Geoff lumbered out of the office, the door swinging closed with a soft click behind him.

Once the echo of his departure faded, Mavis let out a deep breath.

"Well, that was strange!"

"Strange doesn't even begin to cover it," Gemma said in a small voice. "You know Mavis, I'm still not entirely convinced that Geoff's not involved somehow. But I must admit, I'm more inclined to be sympathetic to him after today's conversation."

Mavis nodded thoughtfully. Her gaze lingered on the closed door, as if looking for answers. Shaking off the rising tension, the two women exited the small office and returned to the café.

The members of the chess club were still absorbed in their games of strategy and skill, oblivious to the outside world. Gemma decided to get absorbed in their games, a welcome distraction from the heavier matters that demanded her attention. A young man caught her eye and gestured towards an empty chessboard.

"Care for a game?" he called out, a friendly challenge in his tone.

"Sure, why not?" Gemma replied enthusiastically. She took her place across from him on the table, while Mavis watched.

The young man chose his colours, and then the game began. Gemma's hand hovered over the white pieces before moving her king's pawn forward two spaces. Her opponent countered, and they exchanged a few standard moves in silence. When the moment was ripe, Gemma advanced her left-hand knight's pawn, sacrificing it to gain a lead.

"Ah, ambitious!" her opponent remarked, clearly impressed as he captured the offered pawn.

Gemma smiled, feeling the thrill of the game wash over her. For now, the mysteries and worries of the real world could wait — it was time to focus on the battle of wits unfolding on the chequered black-and-white field before her.

Chapter Twenty-Nine

The following day, after closing the bookstore, Gemma walked across the marketplace to the Coppice carpark, followed closely by a cheerful Mavis making a fuss over the ever-enthusiastic Baxter. Gemma had collected him from the vet and brought him to the shop earlier that afternoon, and Baxter had spent an entire day running around, upsetting the bookshelves and befriending the customers.

"Another busy day conquered," Gemma sighed with satisfaction, climbing into the driver's seat of her trusty VW Beetle. Mavis took up the seat beside her, and Baxter's tail wagged an eager thud against the backseat.

"And quite the triumph with the chess club yesterday, wasn't it?" Mavis beamed.

"Absolutely!" A smile played on Gemma's lips as she

pulled away from the curb. "I could have done without Geoff's little performance, though."

They drove through the picturesque streets of Belper and headed towards the nearby village of Ambergate. A mere ten-minute drive from Belper, Ambergate was a famed beauty spot, a small hamlet nestled in the rolling green fields where the River Amber joined the River Derwent.

"Here we are," Gemma announced as they reached the Holly Lane carpark, which was more a patch of gravel than anything else. It was tucked away right near the start of the famous Betty Kenny walking route, a favourite of dog walkers.

"Baxter's looking forward to a nice long run tonight, aren't you, boy?" Gemma cooed. She released her furry companion from the car, and clipped on his leash. Baxter's nose twitched eagerly at the countless scents that danced on the evening breeze. They crossed the road and joined the path at the start of the walk. Once they were well away from the road, Gemma unclipped his leash and let him roam free.

"Off he goes!" Mavis exclaimed. Her voice rang with delight as she watched the rambunctious dog dart towards the inviting shadows. "He's got the right idea. A bit of fresh air does wonders for one's mind!"

As the setting sun softened the edges of the day, they headed down the path towards the forest, listening to Baxter's joyful barks while he chased squirrels. This was the epitome of tranquillity, the perfect end to an eventful week. It felt as if all three of them breathed in a deep sigh of relief — the pure air cleansed their hearts, and drove away all the cares in the world.

Loose shingle crunched underfoot as Gemma and Mavis continued along the track. Baxter's leash swung from Gemma's hand.

"About Geoff's visit yesterday," Mavis began, "what did you make of it?" Her voice was contemplative, its cadence blending with the evening birdsong.

"It felt— odd, somehow. He seemed quite remorseful about scaring Donna, but who knows if it was just a performance? Feigning remorse in order to obtain our sympathy?" She glanced at Mavis, whose keen eyes reflected understanding.

"Could he really be Dominic's killer?" Mavis asked. "What do you think?"

"I'm not sure," Gemma admitted, her gaze following the trail ahead. "His anger the other night was definitely palpable... but murder? That's a different league of outrage. I can't help but feel that committing a *cold-blooded* murder over a debt would be disproportionate, even for someone with Geoff's temper. I mean, I can imagine him clubbing someone on the head in a fit of rage — but this murder would've required a calm, collected mind, you know?"

As they meandered along the path, conversation ebbed and flowed with comfortable ease. It wasn't long before Gemma circled back to something that had been eating away at her. "Geoff employs a teenager who matches the description of the person seen leaving Dominic's house."

"Ah yes, Ricky, wasn't it? But to be sure, his description *was* quite vague. As Geoff himself said, most teenagers wear hoodies these days. And this boy had nothing to do with the extension or the kitchen work."

Gemma watched Baxter chase a leaf drifting through the air. "That's what Geoff says. Insists Ricky wasn't involved with the extension to Dominic's house. But we only have his word for that."

"Hard to say without checking their alibis," Mavis said, tapping a finger against her lips. "But it seems like a piece of the puzzle that's worth examining."

"Perhaps I should pass this on to David," Gemma suggested. Perhaps her ex-fiancé's admittedly sharp detective skills might make something more of this piece of information. "Weak as it seems, it *is* a lead."

"Couldn't hurt to mention it," Mavis said, nodding. "For all we know, it might be the missing piece that brings it all together."

They descended through the ruins of the abandoned Ambergate wireworks, its rusted girders and hollow buildings spread out like a gallery of industrial ghosts. In its prime, the wireworks would have been a hive of activity, each corner an intricate symphony of clanking metal — now, however, it was merely an echo of a distant past, a symbol of accomplishment vanquished by the ravages of time and nature.

"Imagine," Gemma said, gesturing to the skeletal structures, "this place once competed for the contract to make suspension cables for the Brooklyn Bridge."

Mavis hummed, her gaze travelling over the corroding artefacts of a bygone era.

They continued on their path, leaving the past behind them as the forest — Shining Cliff Woods — welcomed them with open arms. A rich tapestry of lush green unfurled before them, and Baxter, unburdened by the thoughts of history or mystery, darted straight between the trees. His barks filled the air, mingling with the songs of the warblers hidden among the leaves.

"Look at him go!" Mavis chuckled. "Not a care in the world."

"Must be nice," Gemma replied with a wistful smile, watching the brown blur of his coat romp under the cover of ancient sycamores, and bound across the forest floor carpeted with bluebells.

The immense quietude of the woods, punctuated by birdsong and the occasional snap of a twig underfoot, afforded Gemma a moment of introspection. It was Mavis who eventually broke the silence, her soft singsong voice piercing through Gemma's reverie.

"Seeing David again... How did that feel?" she asked, peering at Gemma with those perceptive eyes that missed nothing.

Gemma hesitated, caught off guard by the sudden change in the subject. The cool forest air seemed to press against her skin, urging frankness.

"To be honest, Mavis... I've missed him," she said in a small voice. "All this sleuthing has made me realise just how hard detective work really is."

"Do you regret calling off the engagement?" Mavis prodded gently.

"Maybe... Just a little."

Gemma's confession hung between them. Feeling vulnerable, she brushed a piece of lint from her sleeve. "I keep wondering if I gave up too easily. If I made a terrible mistake."

"Ah," Mavis nodded wistfully. "It's one mystery that's never easy to solve."

Gemma's gaze lingered resolutely on the path ahead. "But maybe it's still worth trying to unravel them."

They resumed their walk, lost in thought, as Baxter scampered ahead. Gemma toyed with the idea of reconciling with David. But their entire relationship now felt as tangled as the brambles that bordered their path. Mavis, sensing her unease, cast a sidelong glance at Gemma. "Why not ask him for a coffee or something? Clear the air, you know?"

"Already floated that idea," Gemma replied, her fingers nervously tracing the worn leather of Baxter's leash. "But I'm involved in this investigation now. He said it would be a conflict of interest."

"Quite the sticky wicket," Mavis said, her lips twitching with amusement. "Looks like we'll have to crack this case quickly then. For the sake of your love life, if nothing else."

"Very funny, Mavis," Gemma said, making a sarcastic face, but her smile was genuine enough.

As dusk approached, they decided it was time to turn back. Baxter, after having dashed through the forest with unrestrained glee, seemed to agree with the plan, his tongue lolling happily.

The two women retraced their steps with a quickened pace, and soon enough, the Ambergate wireworks came into view. The long-forsaken buildings loomed against the twilight sky, the dark, glassless windows looking like hollowed-out eyes. A shiver ran down Gemma's spine. She was about to make a cheeky joke to lighten the ominous atmosphere, when her gaze fell on her dog.

Baxter had halted, his twitching ears perked up and his body tense. He let out a low growl, his gaze fixed on an opening in the nearest building: a ramshackle shell covered in deteriorating corrugated iron sheets, with a sloped, moss-covered roof.

"Something's caught his attention," Gemma whispered, her heart pounding despite her outward composure.

"Probably just a fox, my dear," Mavis reassured her, even as she clutched her cardigan with a trembling hand.

"Maybe." Gemma's voice had none of its usual firmness. Baxter, emboldened by whatever scent or sound had drawn him, darted towards the building, and disappeared into the doorway.

"Wait, Baxter!" Gemma called out, her words dissipating into the evening air. She dashed towards the dilapidated building after Baxter, whose barks had taken on an urgent timbre.

"Baxter, come back!" Her voice echoed against the cold brick.

"Stay here, Mavis," she instructed over her shoulder, not waiting to see if her friend complied.

Gemma entered the old building with caution, her eyes scanning the corners for her dog. The inside of the building felt even more ominous than its forbidding exterior. The ground was covered with mud and decay, and every inch of the walls featured graffiti that would make the vicar blush.

Baxter stood near a corner, hackles raised, snarling at a figure hunched over a small, flickering fire. A hood obscured the person's face, their attention absorbed entirely by the fire.

While Gemma hesitated over the wisest course of action, the figure scrambled to their feet, sending sparks flying dangerously close to their covered face. Baxter lunged forward with a protective ferocity, his bark reverberating into the quiet night.

"Easy, Baxter!" Gemma tried to soothe him, even as

adrenaline surged through her veins. She stood by the sole exit, blocking the stranger's path, further spooking them. Before Gemma could say a word, the figure let out a startled yelp, and in a desperate bid for escape, shoved past her with surprising force.

She stumbled to her side, doing a double-take at the sound — it sounded extremely familiar. Her mind scrambled to place it.

"Stop!" Mavis's voice came from outside, sharp and unexpected against the chaos.

But the figure didn't heed. They disappeared into the twilight, leaving Gemma to gather her wits, her heart racing.

Taking a moment to pull herself together, Gemma made a beeline for the campfire, the residual heat warping the air. She kicked vigorously at the burning items with her sturdy walking boots, sending them scattering onto the muddy floor. One by one, she stamped out the flames, a plume of smoke chasing the embers skyward.

"Come on!" She made an exasperated sound under her breath, almost despairing of success. But the glow eventually subsided, and what was left made Gemma's blood run cold.

The charred remnants were medication boxes labelled *Propranolol*. And beside them lay the half-burnt carcass of a large black hoodie and baggy jeans.

"Oh, my god, this must be the killer!" she whispered, the words barely escaping her lips. The revelation sent a shiver down her spine, and she stared blankly at the floor for a few moments. It was the thought of Mavis outside that finally spurred her into motion. She raced out of the building, her boots crunching over the muddy concrete floor.

"Mavis!" Gemma called out in a shaky voice. "Are you okay?"

Mavis stood a short distance away, silhouetted against the fading light.

"I'm fine, dear," she said, her tone steady despite the consternation in her eyes. "Just a bit startled, is all."

"Did you see who it was?" Gemma asked, hoping for any stray detail that might unveil their identity.

"No, their head and face were covered," Mavis shook her head. "Could have been anyone."

Gemma clenched her fists, frustration boiling inside her. "It was the killer, Mavis. They were trying to get rid of the evidence." She reached quickly into her pocket. "I need to call David."

"Be quick about it," Mavis urged, her gaze fixed on the darkening woods that the killer had sought cover in. "We can't let them get away with this!"

With a brisk, resolute motion, Gemma dialled David's number, the sound of the ring crisp in the hushed evening air. She pressed the speaker button just as he answered.

"David, it's Gemma. I'm here with Mavis," she said

without preamble, urgency sharpening her words. "We're at the wireworks. We've stumbled upon someone — likely Dominic's killer — trying to burn the evidence."

"Are you both okay?" David's voice betrayed an anxiety that wasn't entirely professional.

"We're fine, no need for medical help," Gemma reassured him. "But the person ran off. I kicked some things out of the fire before it all went up — empty boxes of Propranolol, a black hoodie, and baggy jeans."

"Okay, don't touch anything else," David instructed. "I'm on my way."

"Should we stay here?"

"If you can. We don't want anyone tampering with potential evidence. Only stay if it's absolutely safe, though. I'll be there as quick as I can."

The line went dead, plunging Gemma and Mavis back into tense silence. It was Baxter who broke the spell by nudging Gemma's hand with his wet nose.

"Good boy, Baxter," she murmured, stroking his head as they waited.

Half an hour went by before they finally heard the sound of a police car. It came along the pathway to the wireworks. David quickly climbed out of the car, accompanied by another uniformed officer.

"This is Constable Shaw," said David. The police constable nodded at Gemma and Mavis. "Show me what you found."

Gemma led the way into the wireworks building, the charred remains of the campfire still sending up stray wisps of smoke mixed with bits of ash. She pointed out the discarded medication boxes and the scorched clothing.

"Baxter led us here," she explained, watching as David carefully placed each item into evidence bags, "and I saw a figure hunched over a fire, poking at these with a stick."

"These old wireworks," he muttered, sealing the last bag, "always draw in folks looking to hide away. People taking drugs, engaging in all sorts of mischief." He looked into Gemma's eyes with something approaching worry. "You shouldn't be walking here in the evenings."

"We've never had trouble before," Gemma said, though his words unsettled her. "Baxter loves running through the woods."

"Let's just say tonight was an exception," Mavis interjected with a nervous smile.

"You get all sorts roaming here," David said. "Mostly teenagers drinking and smoking."

Gemma nodded, understanding the gravity of their discovery. Their peaceful evening escape had turned into something far more sinister — and potentially dangerous for them.

"Are you parked at the carpark down near the beginning of the walk?" David asked.

"Yes, we are."

"Okay, hop in. We'll drop you off there."

David put the evidence bags in the boot of the police car with meticulous care as the two women climbed into it. Gemma felt both relieved and horrified. She had run into, and almost grasped the murderer, but they slipped through her fingers. For the first time, the sordid reality of this murder case hit her. This wasn't just something to be discussed casually over coffee and flapjacks. It was real, squalid, and terrible.

Constable Shaw started the engine, carefully turned the car around and then drove back down the track to the car park. "We'll get these medicine boxes and clothes logged and sent to the lab," he said.

Gemma nodded. "Thanks for coming out, David," she said, her voice still quavering.

"Of course," David replied. His eyes softened for a moment as they met hers. Then they turned business-like again. "Just doing my job."

A few minutes' drive brought them to the carpark, and they made their way back to Gemma's car, the silence between them reflecting the weight of what they had just witnessed.

"Can you believe all this?" Mavis asked, finally breaking the stillness as the engine hummed to life. She still sounded slightly out of breath. Gemma couldn't be sure if it was from excitement, or trepidation.

"It's like something out of one of our mystery

novels," Gemma said, forcing a half-smile as she navigated out of the car park.

"Except we're living it," Mavis said, shaking her head. Now that the fear and adrenaline had died down, she felt the familiar itch of intrigue beneath her skin. The puzzle pieces were there, but *how* they fit together still remained elusive.

Pulling up to Mavis's house, Gemma turned off the ignition, and looked at her friend. "You sure you'll be alright tonight? I can stay with you, if you wish."

"Oh, I'll be alright, my dear. Nothing like a little adventure to sweeten my sleep. I'll call if I need you."

Gemma smiled at her tenacity. "Make sure you do, Mavis. No matter the hour."

Mavis nodded. "What will you do now? Go home?"

"I have a small hunch I want to follow up on first," Gemma said. "But let's meet at the shop on Monday, unless you ring me first. The hunch is probably nothing, but I won't be able to rest until I check."

"Sounds like a plan, my dear," Mavis said, stepping out of the car. "But please be careful."

"Goodnight, Mavis!" Gemma called out, waiting until her friend walked down the pathway and disappeared inside.

Alone now, Gemma collected her thoughts for a few minutes, before starting the car once more. She drove away, the gears in her mind turning furiously.

Chapter Thirty

Gemma stepped into the Bookworm bright and early the following Monday, after deciding to not open the store over the weekend. Outside, the marketplace was in great spirits, buzzing with activity at the start of the new week. The rising hum of the marketplace filtered through as Gemma prepared the shop for opening. Sarah, the vision of summer in her pink linen frock, had come in early today, and was busy arranging fresh pastries in the glass display case.

"Morning, Sarah!" Gemma greeted her, her eyes fixed on the rows of scones and tarts. "How was Newcastle? Did you have fun?"

Sarah's face lit up. "Oh, Gemma, it was fantastic! We went to this amazing nightclub on Friday — music blasting, people dancing, just electric! And then on

Saturday, we had lunch down by the quayside near the Millennium and Tyne Bridge, soaking in the sun and the sights. After that, it was just bar after bar."

She twirled a lock of hair around her finger, her eyes sparkling with glee as she brightly recounted the details of each establishment they'd stepped in. "And do I have some stories from our bar hopping!" She said with a small laugh.

Gemma nodded along, smiling as she pictured Sarah getting her fill of the vibrant city nightlife.

"Sounds like you had quite the time!" Gemma smiled. "I'm glad you enjoyed yourself. I think I'm far too old for that many bars!"

Before Sarah could launch into another tale, the bell above the door tinkled and Mavis shuffled in, looking energetic and determined as ever. Gemma walked over to her.

"Mavis! Good morning!" She approached the older woman, her features dripping with concern. "How are you holding up after— you know, the wireworks?"

Mavis offered a small smile. "I'm fine, dear. I was a bit rattled at first, to be sure. But nothing a spot of Earl Grey and a few chapters of a comfy book couldn't mend."

Gemma couldn't help but give Mavis an affectionate squeeze. "Well, I'm glad to hear that," she said, smiling warmly. "Now, let's see what the day has in store for us, shall we?"

Together, they took their places behind the counter, ready to greet the eager bookworms for the day.

A few minutes later, Mavis leaned in, the scent of her lavender perfume mingling with the smell of old and new books. "So, did you investigate that hunch of yours?" she whispered, a curious glint in her eyes.

Gemma nodded. "I did. And I think I've figured out who did it."

"What? Who is it?" Mavis's whisper was urgent, her excitement barely restrained as she tightly clutched a new edition of *Murder at the Vicarage* that had arrived in the mail.

"Shh," Gemma cautioned, casting a nervous glance around them. "Not here, Mavis. But I've invited a few people over tonight, after we close. Everything will be revealed then, I hope."

"Like a proper whodunnit reveal!" Mavis exclaimed, clapping her hands. "That's the right way to do it, Gemma!" She patted her friend's arm, with a proud, approving glance.

"Yes, I guess it is," Gemma said, smiling.

She made her way back to the café, where Sarah was precariously balancing two full trays of croissants in her arms, trying to take them out of the oven.

"Sarah, I need a favour," Gemma said, approaching her. "We're having a little last-minute event tonight after closing. Could you stay and help with some refreshments?"

"Of course," Sarah replied, her deft hands smoothing a wrinkle on her apron. "Coffee, tea, and tray bakes — and maybe make a cake?"

"Yes, that sounds good!" said Gemma. A flurry of excitement stirred within her as the hands of the clock inched nearer closing time.

Finally, the last particularly fussy customer departed, and a clicking of heels on the wooden floor announced the arrival of the evening's first guest — Donna.

"Thanks for coming, Donna," Gemma said, offering a warm but tight-lipped smile.

Ellie slipped in at her heels, looking around her warily. Her arms were crossed tightly over her chest, as if braced against a chill that only she could feel. An oversized blue cardigan concealed her growing baby bump. Geoff was next, his colossal frame almost filling the doorway as he muttered a greeting, his eyes taking in everyone present in the room.

"Let's head to the back office," Gemma suggested, leading the way past rows of shelves. "We can talk comfortably in there."

Inside, they saw Mavis, already perched on the edge of a chair with the eagerness of a schoolgirl. She offered a conspiratorial nod to Gemma as the others filed in, taking their seats among the mismatched chairs that Gemma had arranged into a semi-circle.

They had barely settled down when Sarah appeared in the doorway, armed with steaming coffee flasks and an array of cakes that sent a sweet, heady smell swirling through the room. She set them down on a small table, and turned to leave.

"Actually, Sarah," Gemma said, "why don't you stay? You might find this interesting."

Sarah's hand froze on the doorknob for a brief moment. Then, she shrugged and took up a stool at the back, her dress draping around her like the petals of a sunflower in a summer garden.

Donna and Ellie exchanged fearful glances. Geoff shuffled uncomfortably in his seat, and cleared his throat a few times. He leaned towards Donna, his voice barely audible.

"Sorry... For before, you know," he muttered. Before Donna could reply, a delicate cough from Gemma drew everyone's attention.

"Thank you all for coming tonight," she began, feeling the weight of everyone's gaze upon her. Gemma took a deep breath, collected her thoughts, and reinforced her resolve. They'd had enough of secrets and intrigues. It was time to lay it all out on the table. The cosy confines of the Bookworm's back office would be the stage for a denouement that no one would forget.

She stepped forward and stood against the towering

bookshelves that lined the back office, full of stock yet to find its way into the shop. She glanced at each of the faces before her, a confused tableau of apprehension, curiosity, and concealed dread.

"All this started rather innocently when I had the pleasure — or the misfortune, depending on how you look at it — of inviting Dominic Westley here for a reading and signing of his book." Gemma paused, assessing the reactions of her audience. Donna's hands clasped and unclasped in her lap, while Ellie's nervous eyes darted from face to face. "Tragically, Dominic fell ill during the event," Gemma continued, "and despite the best efforts of the paramedics, he passed away in the ambulance. The initial pathology report suggested an overdose, a tragic accident involving the medicine he was prescribed for his heart."

A suffocating tension pervaded the room, and the air itself crackled with unspoken thoughts and wordless questions.

"Of course, at that point, I thought the story had reached its sad conclusion." Gemma watched as Geoff shifted uncomfortably. "That was, until Donna told me about her suspicions at the funeral."

"Suspicions?" Geoff blurted out. "What suspicions?" His usual gruff voice had given way to a hushed tremor.

"Donna told us of her suspicions that Dominic's death was no accident," Gemma said. "That it was deliberate, cold-blooded murder. And she also thought that Ellie was involved." Donna's face hardened, a mixture of regret and resolve lending a sharpness to her normally pleasant features.

It was Ellie who reacted first, her shock palpable as she turned to Donna. "You said *what* about me?" Her voice rose, reaching a crescendo of disbelief and indignation.

"Please," Gemma interjected, polite but imperious, "let's not get ahead of ourselves. I'm simply giving an account of the whole affair, as it unfolded in front of me. This is important."

Ellie and Donna reluctantly sank back into their chairs, even as Donna's disdainful glance conveyed that the tension remained unabated.

Gemma cleared her throat. "Thank you. I promise, everything will become clear soon enough. But first, I want to talk about each of you present here today. Since you are all, to borrow an investigative term, 'persons of interest' in Dominic's death. Please, bear with me," she began, her voice steady despite the flutter in her chest.

"Ellie, I'll start with you."

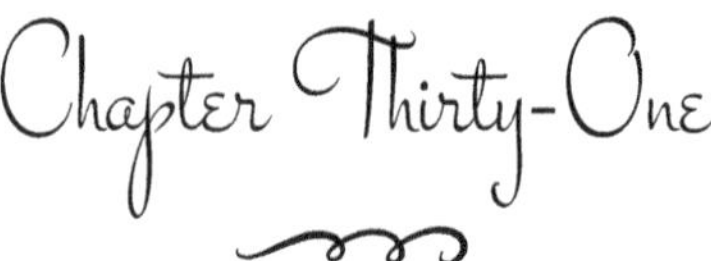

Chapter Thirty-One

Ellie's fingers nervously twisted the hem of her cardigan. "Alright," she finally said, tentative yet defiant. "Let's hear this."

"Donna believes you are the reason her marriage fell apart." Gemma's voice was steady, despite the pounding of her heart.

Ellie's face flushed a deep crimson, and the words tumbled out of her mouth. "That's not true!"

"I know," Gemma said soothingly. "I know that Dominic was already separated when you started seeing each other. So, from that angle, you've done nothing wrong."

"It's true, I haven't! I haven't done anything wrong!" Ellie declared, her voice emboldened by Gemma's reassurance and her own consciousness of the truth.

Donna's eyes widened in surprise. "I— I didn't

know…" she stammered, a faint line appearing between her brows. Her face conveyed utter confusion, followed by embarrassment and remorse.

"However," Gemma added quickly, "that doesn't mean you couldn't have had a motive for killing Dominic, Ellie."

"What?" Ellie gasped. "I didn't do it! Really, I could never!" She looked pleadingly at Mavis. "Why don't you tell her I couldn't…"

Gemma interrupted her with a gesture. "You were in love with Dominic. But your relationship fell apart after you became pregnant with his child."

Donna's head snapped up.

"You're… you're pregnant? And it's Dominic's?" Her voice was almost a squeal.

"Yes, I am," Ellie whispered, her eyes brimming over with tears. She pulled her cardigan even closer, her right hand flying instinctively to her belly.

Gemma looked into the young woman's eyes, and delivered the next words with careful precision. "Dominic, it seems, didn't handle the news of your pregnancy well."

A suffocating silence set in as everyone else seemed to take in this information.

"He made me leave," Ellie cut in, her voice breaking. "And he— he wanted me to get rid of our baby." She stifled a sob.

Donna's hand flew to her mouth. "I didn't know,"

she whispered slowly, as if unable to believe the cruelty of her own thoughts. "Oh honey, that's awful. I'm so sorry. He never told me any of this!"

"Because he's a coward!" Ellie snarled, her eyes suddenly ablaze with fury. Donna could only nod in agreement.

Gemma cleared her throat. "Well, then. If we consider these facts in light of Dominic's death," she said, turning an incisive gaze on Ellie, "then you'd have a pretty good motive."

Ellie's jaw clenched. "I would never do that!" she protested fiercely.

"You lived with Dominic," Gemma continued, undeterred. "Which means you must have been aware of his medical condition, as well as the medication he was on. Technically, you had the opportunity to tamper with them."

"I wouldn't! I— I still hoped that he'd come around to the idea of being a dad! Maybe when he saw the baby, I thought..." Ellie stammered, a flush creeping up her neck. "Besides, I couldn't have tampered with anything! He took my keys, the day I refused to... the day I walked out. I don't have access to the house anymore."

The tension in the room thickened. Gemma noted every twitch, every furtive glance, storing the details like an expert librarian filing away the details of each book in their library.

Geoff shifted his weight again, a creak emanating

from the floorboards beneath him. "Well, it's easy enough to copy keys," he said.

Ellie's eyes snapped towards him. "Not you too!"

"Just saying," Geoff shrugged, giving her a half-hearted smile.

Gemma watched the exchange closely. "Interesting point, Geoff," she said evenly. "But there's more than one side to this story."

She turned to face Donna, who sat ramrod straight in her chair. "Your marriage broke down because of Dominic's affairs — what better reason could there be to harbour resentment?"

Donna's retort came like the crack of a whip. "We were getting back together! I was moving back in with him!"

"So you say. But again, we have only your word for it. What other evidence is there?" Gemma gave her a brisk nod. "While trying to unravel a mystery, one must not take anyone's words at face value. And then there's the matter of your business, which, from what you've told me, is in dire straits."

Donna recoiled, as if stung. "What's that got to do with anything?" She scowled at Gemma, clearly betrayed.

"Everything," Gemma continued in a gentle voice. "Financial strain can lead people to desperate measures. I'm sure all of us are familiar with financial pressures, in one way or another. In fact, keeping the Bookworm afloat has been akin to sailing through a storm. But Donna, after such an extended separation from Dominic, why choose to mend bridges *now*? Could it not seem a little opportunistic?"

"For love!" Donna cried in exasperation, as if the very notion should be beyond question.

"Of course." Gemma nodded. "However, Dominic's successful book and the financial comfort it presumably brought might have been persuasive, for all we know."

Donna scoffed. "Well, his book isn't doing that well!" She gave a hollow laugh.

"Indeed," Gemma said, her tone even. "But we're aware of that fact *only now*, after Dominic has been killed — and after you've examined his accounts."

Donna floundered like a fish out of water, the colour rising to her cheeks. "So you think I did it?"

"Please, Donna," Gemma said, motioning for calm, "I'm not accusing you. I'm merely discussing each suspect's position, as it stands. Scorned by love, yes, but potentially salvaged by a financial lifeline."

Donna huffed, her composed façade crumbling.

"Let's not forget that you knew about Dominic's medical condition, the medicines he took, where he kept them, as well as what an overdose might do," Gemma paused, letting the implications of her words settle in.

"You had the keys, the knowledge, and thus, the opportunity. And your dogged attempts at accusing

Ellie could have been a brilliant piece of misdirection."

The room fell oppressively silent, the ticking of the clock the only sound.

"Okay, alright! I knew about his problems and his medication, but you forget, I wasn't even here when he died. The days leading up to his death, I was in York! The night before at a restaurant, and I drove back the following day, stopping at a service station." Donna looked straight at Gemma. "I told the police all of this. I expect they'll check with all these places. I've told you before, Gemma, I have nothing to hide!"

"I'm sure they'll check your alibi in detail," Gemma said.

Geoff chuckled, highly amused by this domestic drama. "Let's not forget your role in all of this, Geoff," Gemma added sharply.

Geoff's brow furrowed and his amusement disappeared, replaced by a flicker of anxiety. "What about me?" he asked, his voice guarded.

"Your construction firm built Dominic's fancy new extension and kitchen."

"That's right, we did. And what of it?" Geoff challenged, his hands shoved into the pockets of his worn jeans.

"And Dominic left you hanging. Kept putting off the payment he owed you — thirty thousand pounds, wasn't it?"

"Give or take," Geoff grunted, his jaw set. "I just

need what I'm owed. I've got me own bills too, you know! Workers to pay, mouths to feed!"

"Understandable," Gemma nodded, her voice softening slightly. It was hard not to empathise with a man simply trying to keep his business afloat. But, she reminded herself, the man in question was a desperate, short-tempered person, with a history of violence.

"But we can't overlook your history, Geoff," Gemma continued after a little pause. "You've served time for GBH. That's no small matter."

Geoff's eyes hardened. "All of that's behind me. And it's none of your business, to be sure! God knows I've paid for that mistake. I wouldn't risk my freedom over something like this."

"Perhaps," Gemma said, tapping a finger against her chin. "Yet, your demeanour was anything but peaceful the day you stormed into Dominic's house, demanding Donna clear the debt. Gave us quite a fright, I must say."

Geoff glanced at Donna, who was watching him warily. "I've told you I'm sorry for that," he said, reddening all over. "No excuses. It was unacceptable. I just wasn't thinking straight." The words seemed to weigh on him, and he met Donna's gaze with something almost approaching shyness.

Gemma's eyes remained fixed on him, examining his posture, reading his gestures. Was it genuine remorse, or simply an act of self-preservation?

Donna looked at Geoff's surly face, and gave him a sad smile. "It's fine, Geoff. I accept your apology," she said, the tension in her shoulders easing.

As Geoff returned her tentative smile, the atmosphere in the room seemed to shift subtly. The spell of dread and tension seemed broken, with each person seeing the other more clearly, unobscured by lies.

"Geoff, you've stated that Dominic's medical issues were news to you," Gemma said. "Understandably so, since your role was merely to add an extension to his house."

"Exactly," Geoff said, eager to distance himself as far as possible. "And the build finished ages ago. My access to the house was minimal, save for when Dominic was there overseeing the work. Most of the work had to be done outside, until we fitted the kitchen, plumbing and electrics. And Dominic was always there."

Gemma nodded. She turned away from Geoff and walked over to the window, peering out at the alleyway at the side of the store.

"So now we know the suspects — their dynamics with Dominic, their motives, and opportunities. However..." Gemma's voice trailed off as she pondered on the different pieces of the puzzle. Her reflection in the windowpane stared back at her.

"There are still some elements that don't quite fit together. And two details have especially been gnawing at me."

Chapter Thirty-Two

Four pairs of curious eyes followed Gemma's movements as she turned away from the window and sat down on a worn leather armchair in the middle of the office. She cleared her throat, and began.

"First of all, Dominic needed to take a significant amount of the medicine, propranolol, to cause death as per the pathologist's report. At first, we asked the obvious question. Could Dominic have simply hoarded his medication for a while, and then taken it all together to commit suicide?"

She paused for a moment, letting this hypothesis sink in.

"But we soon realised that that was impossible, for several reasons," Gemma continued, taking a deep breath. "First of all, if Dominic did want to commit suicide, why take the overdose right before coming to a public event, when he could have done so at any time? Why go through the convoluted way of taking his own prescription medicine?" She watched her audience nod slowly, as if absorbing the implications of her words, but unable to find a satisfactory answer.

"But what clinched it," she went on, "was when Donna took the police through Dominic's prescription documents. The number of tablets he had roughly matched the documents." She shook her head. "No. Dominic misusing his medication was highly unlikely." Gemma glanced at Donna, who was nodding emphatically. "Moreover," she said, "Dominic certainly didn't have any reason to take his own life. After all, he was due to reconcile with Donna. He did have the debt, but that could easily have been paid off in his head by an uptick in his book sales."

Gemma now leaned over in her seat, glancing around at the assembled faces, all rapt with attention.

"The thing is," she began, her voice low, "acquiring propranolol in the quantity found in Dominic's system presented its own mystery. It's not something you can just pick up at the corner shop, nor is it so easily plucked from the virtual shelves of online pharmacies without a proper prescription or consultation. I checked."

Mavis chimed in with a knowing look. "Yes, indeed. And that stumped us for quite a while, didn't it, my dear?"

"Absolutely," Gemma said, peering through the window into the distance. "We only figured this puzzle out when I invited my friend Jack to upgrade our point-of-sale system, here in the shop."

"Ah, Jack," Mavis murmured absently. "Such a helpful young man!"

Gemma chuckled. "Yes, well, it was Jack who took us into the murky depths of dark web marketplaces, showing us how you could buy anything from narcotics to firearms on online black markets using bitcoin."

"You mean to say," Donna interjected, clearly shocked, "that people actually sell such things on the internet? And how do you get them? The post?"

"Exactly," Gemma said, nodding. "Just like a parcel containing a new bestseller. It's shockingly simple once you know how, and it provided a plausible answer to how our killer could have gotten enough propranolol to..."

"To pull off a murder, and make it look like an accident," Mavis finished grimly.

Geoff scratched his head, bewilderment drawing deep lines on his weathered face. "All this talk of the dark web and bitcoin might as well be science fiction to me," he grumbled. "I can barely turn on a computer without something going wrong!"

"I've heard of bitcoin," Donna chimed in, folding her arms across her chest. "It's all the rage with the younger lot these days. It's like virtual money, isn't it?"

"Give me good old-fashioned cash any day!" Geoff grunted, looking around the room for support.

Mavis came to his rescue. "I said the same thing. Cash is *real.* You know where you are at with it."

Ellie, who had been silently taking in every word, finally piped up. "But surely, the police would've checked up on these possibilities before ruling the death as accidental?" Her brows were furrowed in thought. "You know, the post office could track any of these parcels. I don't know, but there must be some way to find out where they're coming from!"

Gemma shook her head. "Sadly, there isn't," she replied. "It's all very anonymous. Once it enters the postal system, it's just like any other parcel. No red flags raised, no questions asked."

The group mulled over this unsettling reality, each person thinking about how dangerous such a thing could be. Geoff was still incredulous about the whole thing, while Donna and Gemma seethed in silent dismay and indignation. A murder had been committed, and the method was as easy as shopping online!

Gemma deftly steered their thoughts to the other puzzle piece. "So much for the first conundrum of 'how'. Then there's the curious case of the boy in the hoodie."

Her tone carried a hint of intrigue. "Quite a bit of confusion has surrounded him ever since he first appeared, skulking at the back of Dominic's funeral."

"Like how I was hiding out of view?" Ellie retorted, slightly defensive. "I wasn't exactly on the guest list, but I just— I needed closure after everything that had happened between us."

"Yes, Ellie." Gemma looked at her sympathetically. "But we knew your reasons for being there, as did Donna herself. You wanted to pay your respects because of your history with Dominic, and you remained hidden because you didn't want to embarrass Donna." "But who was this boy, and what was his relationship with Dominic?" Gemma's question hung in the air, inviting a series of speculative looks from her audience. "Which leads us to Dominic's next-door neighbour. He spotted someone in a hoodie with their face obscured, leaving Dominic's house the day after his death, early in the morning."

Donna shook her head. "I have no idea who it could have been, or why they'd be there. I can't think of any teenage boy related to Dominic."

"Indeed," Gemma said with a slight tilt of her head. "The neighbour said they seemed calm, not skittish at all. And then, the kitchen... It was scrubbed clean, reeking of bleach," she paused to think. "Was this young man destroying evidence? Crushing up pills to stir into Dominic's morning coffee or mix into his breakfast, perhaps? And if so, for what reason?"

The room fell silent again, each person digesting the implications. "Furthermore," Gemma continued, "this elusive lad must have had an alarm fob. According to the alarm logs, a specific fob was used to set and unset the system that morning, the exit time corresponding with the neighbour's account." She tapped a finger against her chin, looking at the ceiling. "If we find that fob, we might just find our murderer."

Donna gingerly set her coffee cup down. "Well, what are the chances of that happening *now*?"

"That," Gemma said, folding her arms across her chest, "is indeed a good point." She sat back in her chair, the creaking sound slicing through the oppressive silence of the office. "But the fact still stands that that hoodie-wearing youth is the key to all this."

Her eyes scanned the faces before her: Geoff's furrowed brow, Ellie's wide-eyed concern, Donna's dropping jaw. "And it wasn't until last Friday that we had a bit of a breakthrough, when Mavis and I came head-to-head with the potential killer."

"Wait, what?" Donna gasped. "You saw the killer?"

Gemma gave a slow, deliberate nod. "Yes, I believe so."

Ellie leaned forward. "How can you be so sure?"

Gemma let out a deep breath. "Well, last Friday, Mavis and I were taking an evening stroll around Shining Cliff Woods with Baxter. Nothing out of the ordinary." She paused, her eyes glazed over as if she could still see the scene unfold before her.

"On our way back," Gemma continued, "Baxter

heard something." A faint smile appeared at the thought of her faithful companion. "He darted off towards one of those abandoned wireworks buildings."

"And you followed him?" Geoff asked, sceptical.

"Of course," Gemma replied. "It was getting really dark, and the wireworks is an eerie place. But when Baxter bolts, I bolt." She clasped her hands together, remembering the adrenaline that had coursed through her bloodstream. "We went in there and..." her voice trailed off, the image vivid in her memory.

"Go on," urged Ellie.

"We disturbed someone trying to burn something," Gemma said, her voice grim.

The group exchanged anxious glances.

"When they saw me and Baxter, the person yelped and scrambled to escape, barging past me in a blind panic. Mavis, who had been waiting just outside the dilapidated building's entrance, was almost knocked over."

"It was quite scary," Mavis nodded, clutching her cardigan. Her face, however, clearly showed how much pleasure she'd taken in this adventure.

"After they had run off, we approached the flames, and found what they wanted to burn — the remnants of propranolol boxes, half-blackened and distorted by the heat. Fortunately, part of the label was clearly legible. There was also a pair of jeans and an old black hoodie."

"Oh my gosh!" Ellie gave an involuntary gasp.

"I quickly kicked all the items out of the fire and stamped out the flames, and then called David, a Detective Inspector at the Ripley station. He rushed there with one of his colleagues and bagged up the evidence."

"You didn't catch a glimpse of who it was, then?" Geoff asked. His eyes darted between Gemma and Mavis with a blend of awe and trepidation.

Gemma shook her head. "No, but—" she paused, recalling the brief sound that had escaped the fugitive. "There was something familiar about the yelp they made when they ran away."

"But it could have been anyone," Mavis said musingly, intrigued by this little detail.

"Perhaps. But I had a hunch, and I followed up on it over the weekend."

Donna leaned forward. "So, you know who did it?" she pressed, hopeful yet weary, as if she wanted this whole ordeal to end more than she wanted to find out the killer.

"Yes. I believe I do," said Gemma.

Geoff, arms crossed defensively over his chest, chuffed out a hollow laugh. "Well, ladies, it definitely wasn't me!" he declared, as if daring the others to challenge his innocence.

"And it wasn't me either," Ellie echoed, cradling her belly. "I mean, come on, I'm pregnant!" Donna winced at the word 'pregnant'. "I certainly wouldn't be poking about old buildings in the middle of nowhere!"

The Bookworm itself seemed to hold its breath, every eye fixed on Gemma. She scanned their faces. Mavis, Donna, Ellie, and even Geoff, for all his gruff detachment — all four of them hung expectantly onto her every word, their eyes filled with a desperate curiosity.

"So, do you want to know who it is?" Gemma heard a sound behind her.

Chapter Thirty-Three

Gemma stood up from her chair, and looked towards the back of the room, where the young waitress was about to leave through the door.

"Going somewhere, Sarah?" Gemma said. Her face was a pale as a ghost as the colour had drained away. "You've been awfully quiet, my dear!"

Sarah, with a vacant face, smoothed the edges of her usual dress, and shrugged.

"I'm sure this is all quite interesting, Gemma, but excuse my lack of enthusiasm. After all, it has nothing to do with me." She gave a forced smile to the rest of the company.

Mavis was on the point of uttering a reproach, but Gemma forestalled her. "Oh, come now. This won't do," she said with a smile. "It has everything to do with you. You made some pretty big mistakes."

Comprehension dawned on the four eager faces that were fixed on Gemma. Mavis looked at Sarah, her quick mind filling in the blanks of the puzzle, and clucked pityingly. Geoff's jaw dropped and his rough hands clenched unconsciously. Ellie stared wide-eyed at no one in particular, overwhelmed by disbelief. And Donna, whose marriage had been a roller coaster of frustrated love, hope and despair, stared at Sarah, her face oscillating between shock and betrayal.

"The boy in the hoodie has been our biggest stumbling block," Gemma said evenly. "But it wasn't a boy at all, was it? It was you, Sarah, clad in baggy jeans and a hoodie!"

Sarah's quick reply came in an exasperated voice. "This is stupid! Are you saying I look like a boy? You've been reading far too many Agatha Christie novels, Gemma!"

The assembled gathering watched Sarah with bated breath. They still couldn't quite wrap their heads around this lithe young woman being a cold-blooded murderer.

"You know what your biggest mistake was?" Gemma went on, undeterred. "Failing to dispose of the medicine packets promptly." She watched in satisfaction as Sarah stiffened. "There have been several refuse collections since Dominic's death, and yet you kept the boxes.

You probably thought it would be safer to keep them hidden, didn't you? After all, there was no reason to suspect you at all."

Gemma paused. She looked around at everyone, letting each word sink in. "And then, when the walls closed in, you panicked and thought the wireworks would be the perfect place to dispose of the evidence. Remote, dilapidated, and quiet after dark."

The mask of detachment Sarah had adopted began to crumble, bit by bit. She stood up, and clutched the side of the table to steady herself.

"Little did you know," Gemma continued, her unwavering gaze fixed on Sarah, "I often walk Baxter along the trails in Ambergate. It's one of our favourite haunts."

"Ridiculous!" Sarah scoffed, tossing her hair with a practiced air of indignation. "You can't just throw accusations around like this. You have no proof it was me!"

"Ah, but I do," Gemma smiled. "When you were startled in that building by Baxter and me, you let out a loud groan. Distracted as I was by your escape, that sound got me thinking."

Sarah folded her arms, her eyes narrowing. "Oh, yeah? Are you going to tell me that you recognised that one random groan as my voice? What's next, Gemma?" She laughed scornfully.

"You told me you were in Newcastle over the weekend," Gemma said with a small, knowing smile. Each word was deliberate, measured. "Yet, from Friday night through Sunday evening, I kept a watchful eye on your house. Imagine my surprise when I saw you leaving the premises, not once, but several times, over the weekend."

The room was still, save for the soft ticking of the wall clock that seemed to echo Gemma's words. Sarah blanched, seemingly at a loss for words, her confident defiance wavering with this revelation.

"It's curious, you know," Gemma continued, pacing around the room. "When I inquired about your weekend this morning, simply out of politeness, you told me an elaborate rigmarole of names and places. A vivid story filled with minute details." She paused, letting the hint of a smile play on her lips. "You see, one common sign of fibbing is reciting an intricate narrative where a simple answer would suffice."

The group cast furtive glances at each other. Meanwhile, Sarah stood motionless in the corner. Her face had lost its colour, and her bright sundress itself seemed to pale as the truth slowly came out.

Sarah's eyes darted towards the door, her movements slow and deliberate, as if hoping not to draw anyone's attention. Just as her hand grazed the doorknob, the door swung inward. Detective Inspector David Haynes stood in the frame, blocking her escape.

"Not so fast," he said, gentle but incisive.

With a firm hand, he directed her back into the

office, nudging her down onto the chair she had so desperately wished to vacate.

"You have no proof of any of this," Sarah's voice cracked. Her defiance was increasingly tinged with desperation. "So what if I lied about going away? That's not a crime!"

David folded his arms over his chest, leaning against a cabinet. "No, it's not," he said. "But the evidence you tried to destroy is now being examined in our lab." His matter-of-fact tone stripped away the last vestiges of Sarah's bravado.

"Fingerprints, DNA... And the item we found in Mr Westley's ensuite? That'll have DNA on it too."

Sarah recoiled in horror at these last words. She let out a heavy sigh, and her shoulders slumped. The tension in the room was palpable. When she finally broke her silence, her voice trembled.

"Dominic and I," she began, avoiding everyone's eyes, "had been seeing each other on and off for years. It wasn't... We weren't serious. It was just fun — sex."

Donna's hand flew to her mouth, smothering a gasp. Her eyes were wide with shock and anger. Ellie's face turned a shade paler, both women reeling from this matter-of-fact confession.

"It was you," Donna managed to speak, her voice laced with venom, "you're the one who ruined my marriage!"

Sarah tilted her head back and guffawed. "Oh, it

wasn't me! You destroyed your own marriage, you boring old hag!" Her gaze swept over the gathering, resting on Ellie. "And, I wasn't the only one. There were several. Dominic was quite experienced." She smirked.

Ellie's restraint snapped like a twig. "You bitch," she hissed, lunging at her with clenched fists.

But before Ellie could so much as touch a strand of Sarah's hair, Donna put an arm around her and pulled her back. "She's not worth it," she murmured, though her eyes conveyed her own fury.

Mavis, who had quietly watched the drama unfold, spoke up in an accusing tone, "You told us you didn't even know Dominic when we talked about inviting him to the bookshop!" Sarah just gave a careless shrug.

Gemma watched this exchange, wondering how someone so young could harbour such cruelty and duplicity.

"But why kill him? What did he do to deserve that?" she asked. Her voice was calm, almost soft, yet it carried a grave incredulity — as if she couldn't believe *any* reason would justify this heinous crime.

Sarah locked eyes with Donna, her face contorted. "It wasn't just about the sex to me," she said, her voice taking on an edge. "I wanted to be with him. I loved him. And after he dumped Ellie, I thought I'd have my chance."

She paused, a bitter snarl on her face. "But Dominic... he wasn't interested in anything serious with me. And then he had the nerve to say he was putting his affairs behind him! Spurning *me* to get back together with his old hag of a wife!"

Donna shook her head wistfully. "Oh, you foolish child! You don't even understand that it isn't all about age and looks!" She murmured, disgusted.

"Anyway," Sarah continued, "he'd promised to pay for my culinary school diploma. Said it would be an investment in my future!" Her voice wavered. "But when it was time to enrol, he backed out, because 'times were tough'. Still expected me to be his little plaything, though!" She spat.

Geoff had been sitting unobtrusively in the background all this while, too shaken and incredulous to say a word. Now, he came forward.

"And how'd you know all this stuff about medication and that— that dark internet thing?" He was unwilling to believe that a bright, young lass like Sarah could navigate such a sinister underworld.

"Oh, come on!" Sarah snapped with a dismissive wave of her hand. "Anyone under thirty knows about these things!"

Geoff let out a huff, Sarah's words making him feel ancient. "Kids these days!" he grumbled. But there was a hint of jest in his voice, a paltry attempt to inject some humour into the macabre circumstances.

Gemma watched as the different pieces of the puzzle finally fell slowly into place. It was a tale as old as time —

passion, betrayal, jealousy, and a desperate attempt to reclaim control.

"I got the medication because I wanted to make him ill. I just wanted to hurt him; to teach him a lesson." Sarah said. Her eyes darted away for a moment, before meeting Gemma's. "I— I never wanted him dead!" A few crocodile tears rolled down her cheeks. Her hand shook violently as she tucked a stray lock of hair behind her ear.

"Yet the dosage you administered was astronomical," Gemma pointed out dryly. "One doesn't simply stumble upon a coincidentally lethal amount of these tablets without deliberately seeking them out."

Sarah shrugged uncertainly in response. Gemma felt as if the young woman still didn't understand the gravity of illegally procuring drugs and committing murder. It sent a chill down her spine.

"Let me paint a picture for you, Sarah," she continued, her voice steady and business-like. "You stayed over at his house on that fateful evening. And then, in the cold light of dawn, you mixed a lethal amount of propranolol and... slipped it into his coffee? Mixed it in his scrambled eggs, maybe?" Her words hung heavy in the air. Sarah's nod was barely perceptible.

"And he consumed whatever it was you served him," Gemma said, cocking her head, "so there was no stopping the inevitable crash of his blood pressure." Sarah had given up denying the facts Gemma laid out.

"The next morning you slipped back into Dominic's house, clad in an oversized hoodie and baggy jeans, covering your face and womanly features. A spectre intent on erasing her tracks."

The floorboards creaked as Gemma paced around the room. "Except you made truly basic errors," she added. "First, there was the matter of the key fob used to disable the alarm system. A clever touch, save for the fact I'm willing to wager it's still sitting pretty in your house."

Sarah's shoulders sagged as she realised that she'd missed discarding the key fob.

"Then there was your bleach bonanza," Gemma went on, "enough to clean a small hospital. But you went a bit overboard. There were bleach stains on the hoodie you tried to burn. You also overlooked another tiny detail — the used condom in Dominic's bathroom bin." At the last words, Sarah's hands flew to her face in an outpouring of sorrow. "It was a plan executed with cunning, but even the best-laid plans can come undone through the simplest of oversights! Your deviousness had us all fooled," Gemma went on, her eyes not leaving Sarah's defeated form. "Had it not been for Donna's initial suspicion, misdirected though it was, you might have got away with it."

Donna turned to Ellie, her eyes brimming over with empathy and contrition. "I'm sorry, Ellie," she said quietly. "I was just so upset, I wasn't thinking straight.

I've been so cruel to you, and after everything Dominic did too..."

Ellie brushed away the apology with a warm smile. "Don't worry about it, Donna," she said in a soft voice, "I understand."

Gemma looked at David, who was still standing by the door, coolly detached. Catching her eye, David gave her a knowing smile, as if turning the page over their shared ordeal. He stepped forward with a finality that only a man of the law could muster.

"Sarah Hastings..." he began, his voice firm and authoritative.

But before he could finish, Sarah stomped hard on his foot. David gave a loud grunt of pain, and the young woman shoved past him with a surprising burst of energy, escaping into the tranquillity of the empty bookshop.

A cacophony of startled exclamations and the sound of frantic footsteps followed, even as Gemma and the others remained frozen in stunned silence. It was a momentary lapse, broken as a police constable marched a handcuffed Sarah noisily back into their midst. David shook his head in annoyance, and cleared his throat.

"Sarah Hastings, you are under arrest for the murder of Dominic Westley. You do not have to say anything. But it may harm your defence if you do not mention when questioned something which you later rely on in court. Anything you do say may be given in evidence."

As David recited the police caution with a practiced rhythm, Sarah started sobbing, all her bravado sluiced away.

"Take her to the station," he instructed the two officers waiting by the door, who nodded and escorted Sarah to the exit.

David straightened his tie, and turned to Gemma with a nod of solemn respect.

"That was very impressive, Gemma," he said, his eyes twinkling in awe of her. "We'll be searching Sarah's flat for any additional evidence — the key fob, laptops, anything that could further incriminate her. My team will also handle the fingerprint and DNA analysis. Paperwork awaits, I'm afraid."

Gemma nodded, slumping down in her chair. She felt exhausted to the bone.

"Before you drown in paperwork," Gemma called out, stopping him in his tracks, "how about that drink sometime? You know, since it's not a conflict of interest any longer." A playful challenge sparkled in her eyes.

David smiled. "I'd like that very much, Gemma. But I need to get this arrest registered for now." With that, he left Gemma amidst friends who were still reeling from the revelations of the evening.

Gemma turned to her companions. Mavis clasped her hands together, her eyes alight with undisguised admiration.

"Oh, my dear! That was absolutely brilliant! Just like

on the tele," she said, beaming, as if they had all stepped right out of a BBC crime drama.

Donna rose from her chair, relief and gratitude etched on her features. She wrapped Gemma in a heartfelt embrace.

"Thank you," she whispered softly, her voice ringing with a newfound hope. She pulled back, her expression softening as she faced Ellie. "I— I never even knew about the baby, Ellie. I'm so sorry. I can't imagine..." her voice trailed off. "Dominic never even told me. How could he be so callous? Did he think I'd never find out?" She extended her apologies and her genuine concern as an olive branch, anxious to repent for her cruelty as well as offer support to the younger woman.

Ellie accepted the gesture and the hug that followed, her own anxieties unspooling. "Let's put it all behind us, Donna," she murmured, the prospect of a true friendship blooming in place of past hurt.

Vowing to mend more than just her own heartache, Donna approached Geoff.

"I'm selling the house, Geoff. You'll get every penny owed to you," she promised, extending a resolute hand.

"Thank you," Geoff replied, his voice gruff with emotion, hand enveloping hers in a solid handshake.

Chapter Thirty-Four

Gemma was busy scanning new arrivals for the science fiction and fantasy section into the point-of-sale system, when the postman bustled into the bookshop.

"Morning, Lee!" she said, unable to hide the eagerness in her voice. Lee, a portly fellow with a cherry-red face, doffed his cap and handed her a small stack of letters. Hopefully, it would contain the one she'd been waiting for.

"It's a lovely morning, eh?" Lee replied.

"It certainly is," Gemma beamed, thankful for a day that would contain no murderers or sleuthing or clues. Only one week had passed since that fateful evening when Sarah was arrested, and for once, Gemma was glad for the quiet languor of the Bookworm. She had come to truly appreciate the peace of uneventful days.

As Lee exited the store to continue his rounds, Gemma thumbed through the envelopes. She paused at one that was thicker than the rest, and positively official-looking. She held it aloft, a grin spreading across her face.

"Mavis, come look! This could be the one!" Gemma exclaimed, waving the envelope in the air.

Mavis peered over her spectacles from a corner in the romance section. The past few days had been low on excitement, compelling her to revisit her guilty pleasure, *Wuthering Heights,* during slow hours in the shop. "Well, don't just stand there waving, my dear. Open it!"

Sliding her letter-opener through with a quick motion, Gemma ripped open the envelope. Her smile widened — it was the much-awaited alcohol license, granting them permission to serve drinks in the café.

"It's here, Mavis! It's finally here!"

"Brilliant news!" Mavis clapped her hands together, unable to contain her excitement. This would be the start of a new era for the Bookworm! She walked over to the counter and took Gemma's hands in hers. Both women were overwhelmed with glee.

After their initial elation settled, Mavis leaned forward. Her mind was already swarming with possibilities. "You know, Gemma, we could do something really special with this! Imagine... we could expand the café, add some plush reading nooks!"

Mavis swept her hands through the air at the café

with a flourish, like a magician about to make their assistant disappear behind a curtain. "Picture this: people nestled in cosy reading chairs with their favourite books, sipping on a glass of red, lost in other worlds!"

Gemma's gaze drifted to the back of the building. The idea sent a shiver down her spine. This was *precisely* what she'd always wanted the Bookworm to be like!

"Oh, it sounds amazing, Mavis! But an extension would cost quite a lot of money, and all things considered, I'm not sure I could afford it right now."

"True," Mavis nodded. "But you must plant a seed to watch it grow, you know. And I have a feeling this could bloom into something wonderful, my dear."

"I think you're right," Gemma said, her mind abuzz with images of picturesque corners filled with bibliophiles and wine connoisseurs alike. The dream caused flutters in her chest.

Mavis's eyes twinkled. "You know, I've been mulling something over..." she began, intertwining her hands atop the counter with a grim resolve.

"Go on."

"Since my retirement, and poor dear Fred's passing," Mavis said, her voice bittersweet, "I find myself rather flush. Savings here, investments there. And I'd like to put some of it to good use." Gemma tilted her head questioningly, not quite following her.

"Gemma, my dear, I'd like to invest in this place!" Mavis declared gesturing around herself.

"You— you want to be a partner?" Gemma stammered in disbelief.

"Yes, why not? I think I could really help expand the business!"

A flood of emotions swelled within Gemma, disbelief, joy, and relief all jostling for space. Her mouth opened, closed, then opened again. Finally, she managed a breathy, "I wasn't expecting that!"

Mavis nodded so vigorously that her pearl earrings swung about. "We could look at extending the café. Broaden the Bookworm's horizons, you know, offer more than just books and a quick cuppa. We could host evening events, wine tastings, author signings. We must create a community space, Gemma. A hub for culture and comfort, a safe-haven for literary adventure seekers!"

The vision Mavis had painted felt vibrant and alive, and it stirred a rush of excitement within Gemma. She could already envision the comfy chairs filled with customers lost in pages, the soft clinking of glasses accompanying quiet conversations. She imagined people gathering around on a Saturday evening, sampling fine wines, or new brews from local breweries. The possibilities were endless.

"I think it's an interesting idea," Gemma said, nodding slowly. "Let's discuss it over a glass of wine this evening, Mavis. Let's really think it through, come up with a plan, and look at the terms." She reached out across the counter, grasping Mavis's hand in a firm, earnest shake.

Together, they stood behind the counter, hopeful and jubilant — two friends standing together, planning to embark on a new chapter of their lives, their eyes filled with plans and dreams. Their reveries were interrupted by the bell above the front door. They looked up to see David step inside.

"Hello, David," Gemma said, her eyes lighting up. David smiled at her.

"I'm here to give you both an update on Sarah's situation."

"Of course." Gemma motioned towards the café. "Let's take this to somewhere more comfortable, shall we?"

The three of them walked over to the café. Emily, one of the café assistants, appeared at their side, pencil poised over her notepad.

"What would you all like?" she asked with a bright smile, her enthusiasm unabated even though she had to shoulder all the responsibilities alone after Sarah's ignoble exit.

"Skinny Latte for me, please," said Gemma.

"I'll have an Earl Grey, dear," Mavis smiled.

Emily looked at David. "Black Americano for me, please," he said.

"Coming right up!"

"Thank you, Emily," Gemma replied, trying to

mirror the girl's cheery disposition. Emily returned soon, bearing a tray of steaming drinks. She distributed them, and left just as unobtrusively as she had arrived.

"Right then," David began, "here's where we stand with the case." Gemma curled her fingers around her mug, drawing comfort from its warmth, as David leaned forward with a serious expression. "We've been through Sarah's house. Recovered her laptop. You won't believe this — her search history showed she went directly to a bitcoin exchange to transfer money. And the technicians in our lab said she had the Dark Web TOR browser installed, so it's safe to say she knew what she was doing, although she used a regular browser to setup the bitcoin exchange and pay money into it. Quite careless, really."

Mavis, who'd been sipping her tea, set her cup down with a clink. "Bit of an oversight for someone trying to cover their tracks, isn't it? I thought the whole point of bitcoin was that it was anonymous."

"Exactly," David said. "She was really careless. If she'd already had a bitcoin exchange account set up with money in it, it would have been harder for us to see what was happening. But she set up the account and paid in the funds right before buying the medication. It isn't too difficult then to put two and two together."

Gemma shook her head.

"Careless indeed," Mavis muttered, a frown creasing her forehead.

David continued, "Then we did a DNA test on the

contraceptive found in Dominic's bathroom. It was a match for Sarah."

"As we expected," Mavis stated flatly.

"We combed Dominic's whole house and found ample proof once we knew what to look for. Hair in the bathroom, and fingerprints in the kitchen too," David added. "Her bleach cleaning spree wasn't as thorough as she thought, after all."

Gemma pictured Sarah, always so pleasant and cheery with her colourful summer dresses and her serene smile. She could still envision her talking mildly to the customers, chatting with the café regulars and whipping up her special Victoria sponge. And now, this web of evidence painted a completely different portrait. She let out a weary sigh.

"Oh yes," David went on, "we've also spoken to the ladies she was supposed to be in Newcastle with the other weekend." He met Gemma's gaze. "They said Sarah had cancelled that morning, told them she was unwell. It fits with your testimony, Gemma. She must have realised the net was closing in. We suspect she panicked, and desperately started destroying the evidence. People make silly mistakes under pressure."

"That little stakeout of mine turned out to be quite helpful, then?" Gemma said.

"More than you realise," David replied, giving her an impressed smile. "It was what broke her down, knowing she'd been caught in a lie and had no alibi."

"Has Sarah been interviewed further?"

David hesitated, measuring his words. "I can't pass on all the details, to be honest. But I'll tell you this — it's pretty much a cut and dried case when it goes to trial."

"Will it be a long prison sentence?" asked Mavis.

The question lingered heavily in the air, as the two women looked hesitantly at each other. It was almost as if, sitting in the café in the cold light of day, they still couldn't believe Sarah had done all of that.

"Yes, quite a long sentence," David replied. "At least 15 years, I would expect. Whatever the motive might have been, it wasn't exactly a crime of passion in the heat of the moment, you know. It was a calculated, cold-blooded murder, premeditated with another degree of deviousness. It'll definitely be a first-degree charge."

Gemma shook her head. There was a dull ache in her heart, despite the betrayal and lies. "Foolish girl!" she groaned, more to herself than to the others. "What was she playing at?"

Mavis reclined in her chair. "If she didn't want to do the time, she shouldn't have done the crime." There was something ruthless about her nonchalant shrug.

David smiled at the remark. "It would save me a lot of time and paperwork if all criminals thought of that beforehand. Sadly, they all assume they'll get away with it, until it spirals out of their control. And it always does, sooner or later."

He got up and shook hands with Mavis, bidding a polite farewell.

Gemma accompanied him to the door. “Speaking of time,” she ventured, a hopeful upswing in her voice, “how about going for that drink this weekend?”

David’s eyes brightened. “That would be great!” His voice was no longer the authoritative, business-like drawl of the detective. It was the soft, excited assent of a schoolboy. “How about we do dinner at the same time? Can’t drink on an empty stomach now, can we?”

“I’d like that,” Gemma said, standing in the doorway as David climbed into his car. “It’s a date!”

As David drove away, Gemma’s heart did a little skip. *Did I just call it a date*? she thought, smiling from ear to ear.

Chapter Thirty-Five

Sitting at the counter, Gemma chewed the end of her pencil, trying to concentrate on her sketch, a notepad clutched tightly in her hand. Several weeks had flown by since Sarah's arrest, and normalcy had gradually returned to Belper. Tucked in a corner of the marketplace, the Bookworm was buzzing with plans for renewal.

Gemma tried her best to sketch designs for the expansion of the shop. She'd never been one for art, so her drawings were crude, but they outlined her grand visions for the shop and café practically enough.

"Imagine this," Mavis began from a nearby corner, gesturing towards the space at the back of the café, "a comfortable reading area, over there. Oh, and we must have those plump, overstuffed armchairs. You know, the soft ones that swallow you whole. Oh, and table service

— just ring a little bell, and voila! Tea or coffee, or even a nice glass of wine, at your beck and call, without ever having to leave your literary cocoon!"

Gemma smiled at her enthusiasm. "Sounds divine! We could design it like a Victorian library too! With panelled walls and those brass lamps casting a warm glow over everything?"

"Exactly!" Mavis clasped her hands together in a giddy manner. "It's all about atmosphere! Not like these modern libraries, with boring beige walls and sterile white lights. Ours will be a reader's paradise — warm, personal, and tucked away from the world!"

Gemma's head snapped up as the doorbell chimed. Turning towards the door, she blinked in surprise. Ellie, Donna, and Geoff stood on the threshold. Their presence at the Bookworm felt like an unexpected plot twist.

"Ellie... Donna... Geoff..."

Gemma still hadn't forgotten the sensations of the last time these three had been in the same room. She could still feel the tension that had hung thick in the air that day, pervasive like thick dust in an abandoned attic. But now, they sported warm smiles.

"Hello, Gemma!" Donna said brightly. She motioned at an empty table between the bookcases. "Can we have a word?"

"Of course."

Gemma led the way. As they settled down, Gemma couldn't help but marvel at the change. Clearly, the

Bookworm wasn't the only thing undergoing a transformation. The unlikely trio exuded a sense of camaraderie that was as baffling as it was heart-warming, given their tumultuous and conflicting history.

"How are you all getting on?" Gemma asked, curious about this unexpected turn of events.

"Much better, thank you," Geoff answered with a warm smile, as Ellie and Donna nodded in agreement. His gruffness had all but vanished.

Gemma's detective instincts reared their head again, as she wondered what could have bridged the gap between grief and grudges. But for now, seeing the three of them united with some unspoken understanding, Gemma stifled her curiosity. Instead, she let a wave of relief wash over her.

Donna leant forward, her hands clasped together on the worn wooden table. "I've sold the house," she announced flatly, as if she were discussing the weather, and not disposing of a significant piece of marital history.

"I'm sorry you had to do that," Gemma said. But she understood that selling the house was more of a liberation for Donna, than a loss.

Donna waved off the sympathy with a flick of her wrist.

"Oh, no, it's fine, really. After all the... activities that went on there." There was a palpable relief in her eyes.

"Besides," she continued, "the sale was quick. The

buyer wasn't caught up in a long chain." She glanced over at Geoff, who had been following the conversation with interest.

"And about Geoff and his outstanding payments," Donna said, tilting her head in his direction, "I've settled the debt." Her statement hung in the air, the final note on a dispute that had once seemed insurmountable.

"That's excellent news!" Gemma cried.

Geoff responded with a broad, grateful smile. "Much appreciated," he mouthed. The words were laconic, but they conveyed a genuine appreciation and happiness.

Donna hesitated and turned to Ellie. "I've been carrying a lot of guilt," she began in a hesitant whisper, "for accusing you of Dominic's death." She paused, taking a deep breath that seemed to have a calming effect on her. "But I see now, it wasn't your fault that our marriage fell apart. You had nothing to do with it."

Ellie's expression softened, tears brimming in her eyes.

"And what he did to you — finding out about the baby and still..." Donna's words trailed off, her voice filled with sympathy and regret.

"Ellie, I'd like to give you £30,000 from the deal on the house, to help with the baby. You deserve it, considering what Dominic did to you... and really, you know, he should have taken the responsibility, provided for you and the baby."

A collective gasp filled the café, but Donna pressed on. "And I want to be there for you both. You shouldn't have to do this alone."

Ellie's eyes widened in surprise. But a warm smile soon replaced the shock. "We've become quite good friends since Sarah's arrest," Ellie turned to Gemma, by way of explanation.

"That's very nice of you, Donna," Mavis said. "It's the right thing to do."

Gemma looked at Mavis, who gave her an imperceptible nod. She turned to Ellie. "While we're all here, I should mention that the café needs someone to take over from Sarah," Gemma said with a smile. "Ellie, would you help us run the café? I mean, it'd be better to work in a small, friendly café instead of a large, impersonal chain, wouldn't it?"

Ellie hesitated. "It does sound lovely," she confessed, "but the baby is due soon."

"That's fine," Gemma reassured her. "You won't be alone, you know."

Mavis nodded. "You have plenty of friends to support you here at the Bookworm, my dear."

Ellie looked at all of them in turn, her eyes glistening with tears. "I... I'd like that very much."

Gemma's heart swelled with pride. The Bookworm was bringing people together, just as she had always wished. Their being here was a testament to the tight-knit community it had formed, even amidst the darkest of circumstances.

Her gaze shifted from Ellie's tear-streaked cheeks to Geoff, who was silently watching the exchange with folded arms. She cleared her throat. "Mr Dunsworth," she began, "we may have some work for your company, too."

Geoff straightened up, his eyebrows raised in surprise. "Oh! What do you mean?"

"Once we secure permission from the council, we're planning to expand the café," Gemma explained, gesturing towards the back wall. "Would your company be able to draw up a quote?"

A wide smile broke out on Geoff's face. "I'd be delighted to!" He positively beamed. "To tell you the truth, I've been itching to work on something positive after— well, you know."

"Brilliant!" Gemma clapped her hands, looking around at four delighted faces.

Chapter Thirty-Six

The morning light filtered in through the front window, illuminating the dust motes dancing in the air. Gemma was manning the counter, perched upright on her usual high stool, bending over a particularly difficult clue in that day's crossword. Mavis was beside her cradling a porcelain cup, steam curling up from her Earl Grey.

A customer walked into the store, casually making his way to the nearest shelf. He moved through languidly, his fingers trailing over the spines, without actually picking up any one of them. Gemma leaned closer to Mavis.

"Psst, Mavis look! It's him again — the browser who prefers to come over here and buy books online."

Mavis glanced up from her tea. "The nerve of some people!" she mumbled.

Gemma nodded in silent agreement, watching as the man picked out a title and flipped it open. She knew the routine only too well — the quiet rustle of the pages would be followed by the soft clicking of a finger on a smartphone, then a comparison of the prices, and finally the inevitable click of "Buy Now". And despite all this, an unspoken expectation hung in the air, as always, a shared hope that perhaps this time the outcome would be different.

The man made his way to the mystery section, a particularly cosy corner of the shop where shadows played against the rows of shelving. He browsed for a few minutes, and eventually plucked out a hardback from its perch. The glossy sheen of the cover caught the morning light as he thumbed through the pages.

With a smirk, Mavis gently elbowed at Gemma's arm. "Watch him. That phone will come out any second now to check the online price."

But they were to be sorely disappointed. The man simply tucked the volume under his arm and reached for another, a paperback this time. He flipped it open, his eyes scanning the text with an intensity that spoke of genuine interest.

Gemma exchanged a look with Mavis. "Well, that's a surprise! Do you think he might actually buy a book this time?"

"I don't know. Maybe?" Mavis shrugged.

A quarter of an hour trickled by, but the man

continued his exploration. One book became two, then three, and then four, until half a dozen titles were cradled in his arms. Gemma watched, surprised.

With a small tower of books balanced precariously on his arm, the man approached the counter.

"Good morning!" He said cheerfully.

"Good morning," Gemma replied, reaching for the barcode scanner.

"I read about your crime-solving antics in the local newspaper," he said with undisguised admiration. "It was really impressive how you figured out who killed that writer fellow!"

Gemma couldn't help but chuckle as she entered the last book into the point-of-sale system. "Well, to tell you the truth, it's the effect of good company," she said, smiling and nodding towards the murder mystery section. "Those shelves are chock-full of crime fighting stories. They're my how-to guides!"

She slid a voucher across the counter. "Here's a little discount for the café, if you fancy a drink!"

"Actually," he beamed, gathering his new acquisitions, "I think I'll treat myself to a spot of brunch." With that, he picked up his books and strode towards the café, tucked away at the back of the store. Gemma watched him go, the corners of her eyes crinkling with amusement. She turned to Mavis.

"I wasn't expecting that."

The End

Gemma and Mavis will return in Book two - *A Murder at the Church*

Thank you for reading *The Bookshop Mysteries: A Bitter Pill*. We would be grateful if you could leave a review for this book at the store you purchased it. Reviews really help authors. Thank you.

Join the Reading Club

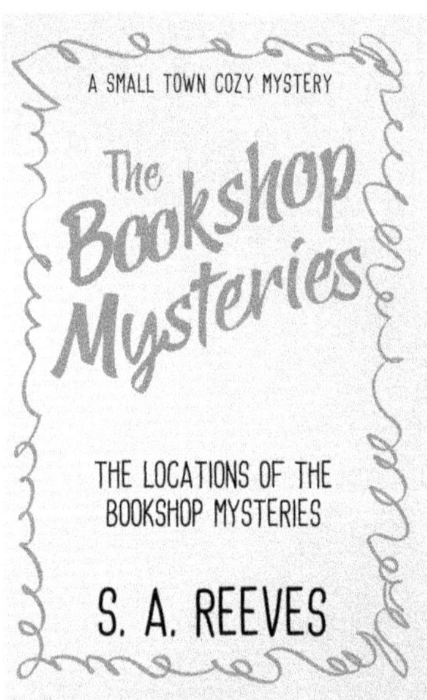

The Bookshop Mysteries is set in a real town, Belper (Derbyshire) in the United Kingdom, and is set in real locations. If you would like to see what these locations look like, then you can join our reading club to receive a free book: The Locations of the Bookshop Mysteries.

By joining the club we will let you know about new releases, special offers, and exclusive behind-the-scenes details about how we write the books.

https://www.sareevesfiction.com/join

The Bookshop Mysteries

Love the Bookworm Bookshop and Café? You can buy exclusive merchandise with the Bookworm's logo, from mugs, bags, t-shirts, hoodies and more.

Order from http://sareevesfiction.com
or scan the QR Code.

www.ingramcontent.com/pod-product-compliance
Lightning Source LLC
LaVergne TN
LVHW052158160125
801516LV00014B/353

* 9 7 8 1 0 6 8 7 2 0 9 3 2 *